TEMPTATION RANCH

JODI PAYNE

BA TORTUGA

Temptation Ranch
Copyright © 2021 by Jodi Payne & BA Tortuga

Edited by LC Hinson

Cover illustration by AJ Corza
http://www.seeingstatic.com/
Cover content is for illustrative purposes only and any person depicted on the cover is a model.

ISBN: 978-1-951011-54-3

Published by Tygerseye Publishing, LLC, July, 2021
Printed in the USA

To our wives.

1

—————

"Tad! Tad, we're over here, man!"

Tad had just arrived, and his eyes were still adjusting to the low light in the bar, but he knew that voice well. His Friday night crowd was here and ready to party, and he was all in. He needed a beer first though, so he pointed to the bar, and Cooper gave him a thumbs up. A shot and a beer, and then he'd pump some money into the jukebox.

His Friday night crowd was all about putting the work week behind them, getting drunk and getting laid, and that was his expectation: to blow off some steam, get stupid, and find someone to take him home.

Sheila was behind the bar, hair up in a messy bun, her T-shirt with the faded Guns and Roses cover on it just tight enough to get attention. "Tequila and a Shiner?"

He nodded to a guy sitting at the bar and then smiled at her. "Man, I come here too often."

"Jack and Coke." Sheila sat the drink down on the bar in front of the cowboy and pulled down a bottle of tequila.

"Thank you, ma'am." Oh, that voice was slow and rough,

like honey poured over river rocks. He took his ball cap off and tucked it in his pocket, then leaned an elbow on the bar. He did come here too often. Every Friday night and the occasional Monday through Thursday if he was bored, but he didn't recall that voice; he'd have remembered it.

"Tad!" He'd just been about to introduce himself when Cooper came over, cheeks glowing and eyes a little liquid. Someone had gotten quite a head start. "What is taking so long?"

"I need a beer, bud. Give me a second."

Cooper hung on him and licked his ear. Did he want Cooper tonight? He'd been thinking maybe Rory. Cooper was sweet and a ton of fun, but usually only good for one round. Rory was heavy-handed and liked to draw things out, keep him up half the night.

"Oh, Coop. Quit hanging on the man and let him have his drink." Sheila set a shot down and his beer beside it.

Cooper pulled back without arguing but pouted, lounging on a barstool beside him. "Bossy."

"Never change, Sheila." Mmm. Bossy. Yeah, he set his mind on Rory. He picked up his shot, swallowed it down with salt but skipped the lime, going right for his beer instead.

He glanced back over at Pretty Voice, finding a crisp white button-down shirt, a gray cowboy hat that cast a shadow, and one large, tanned hand with a gold nugget ring. Okay, that was fine as hell.

Fine. Listen to him. How long had he been living in Austin now? Three years? Or, well seven if he counted his time at UT. He was losing Jersey and gaining words like "fine" and "y'all". And his friends in both states teased him about it every chance they got.

Still, fine was what it was about, wasn't it? Guys in hats

like that, hell not even as nice as that one, were the main reason he'd stayed here after he'd finished school. That, and he had no intention of ever working for his dad.

Oh, and the music. He loved all the live music.

But mainly it was the cowboys.

"Okay, come on, baby." Cooper got an arm around his narrow waist and tugged him right off his stool like he weighed nothing. He took another gulp of his beer and then dragged it off the bar as Cooper hauled him across the room.

"Hey, Tad!" Half the crowd called his name at once, and he held up his beer, but he kept one eye on the bar.

Oh. Wrangler butt. Nice.

He swore that he could see the cowboy's gaze following him all the way to their table.

What was the universal sign for stay right there, and I'll come say hi in a bit? Was there one? He was still working that out when someone took his beer.

"Hey, sugar."

Oh. Rory. "Hey, there. That's my beer."

"Uh-huh." Rory took a sip without losing eye contact and handed it back to him. Damn, that was hot. Rory must be thinking what he'd been thinking because he couldn't seem to look away all of a sudden. "Mmm. Shiner."

"My go-to."

"I know. Come sit." Rory gestured to a chair at the end of the table, and he sat, making room beside him.

"You think the cowboy at the bar knew what he was walking into?" Cooper asked. "This is *not* his crowd."

He looked over at the bar again; he'd take any excuse at this point. "I don't know. What brings a man like that into this part of town anyway?"

"Oh, that's a good game." Rory slid a hand into his hair

and tugged just a little. "Maybe he's investing in something. Building another strip mall."

"What? God, Rory. Use some imagination. He's looking for someone who owes him money and was told the guy would show up here."

Tad snorted. "He's...brooding. He had a bad breakup, and he needs to be where his friends won't find him."

"Ooh. I like that one." Rory gave his hair a playful tug and let him go.

Juanito snorted. "He's trolling for blowjobs, *ese*. You can tell by the boots."

"Yeah?" Cooper grinned wide. "Well, if that's what he wants then he is in the right place after all!" That got a laugh from all of them.

He wondered if it mattered that he was hoping Cooper was right. He wasn't sure he was going to be able to break away from everybody—from Rory in particular—long enough to even get the cowboy's name.

Sheila poured the cowboy another round, laughing at something he said. He pushed money across the bar, and that made her smile even bigger.

All right, Pretty Voice was staying.

"TGIF!" Rory's deep voice growled, and they all clinked beer glasses.

"Long week?" He asked first, so nobody would ask him.

"You wouldn't believe it if I told you." Rory said that every time someone asked. He worked in the prosecutor's office, and he always had good stories. He was right too. Tad almost never believed him. People were crazy.

"Mine was fine. The rush is over for another semester. Shit, why I became a financial aid administrator is beyond me." Cooper grinned over, eyes catching the swirling lights. "Who's drunk enough to dance with me?"

More dancing, less talking. He tipped his beer back and chugged down the second half, then slammed it down on the table. "Me. Soon enough." Not really, but he wanted to dance anyway. Coop was pure sex on the dance floor. And Rory liked to watch.

Cooper took his hand, and Tad followed willingly, right out into the middle of the floor where the lighting was purple.

The music thumped, the floor vibrating with the sound. Cooper grabbed him, writhing against him like a slut, and damn, it felt good.

He was happy to play with Cooper and enjoy a little of the buzz from his tequila. This was what Friday nights were for. And then tomorrow, like nearly every Saturday night, he'd hit a different kind of bar and see if anyone was looking for a boy like him.

Cooper covered one ass cheek with a hot hand, and he looked up, and then toward the edge of the dance floor to see if Rory was watching. Rory was kissing Juanito, but the cowboy? That one was watching him like a hawk.

Damn, had he lost Rory? What were the chances that cowboy would leave the barstool? It seemed like the man might be happy to sit there and watch him all night. Well, he could have fun with that, show off a little, build a little steam under that gray hat. He made a point of staring back, and then turned his attention back to Cooper.

"Rory's just trying to make you jealous, rev you up, man." Cooper licked his ear, bit his earlobe. "We'll give him something to watch."

"You just like showing off." He liked Cooper's brand of flirting, and he liked that his buddy seemed to get that he wanted more than something sweet tonight. He let Cooper handle him a little, spin him, pull him in close, kiss him quick and hard enough to make him blink. He smiled. "You're drunk, Coop, huh?"

"I'm not hurting, honey, but I'll remember this in the morning."

"When Rory takes me home, I'll make sure you get into a cab." He kissed Coop on the cheek. He thought Cooper was the closest he had to a best friend. They'd tried being more, but neither of them was enough for the other that way. It didn't stop them from taking advantage of some benefits now and then, though.

"You're a good guy. I wonder if the pretty cowboy dances?"

"Nah. Not here. He's a two-step guy, don't you think? Isn't that how that type rolls? He drinks Jack and Coke. That's all I really know about him." *That, and he's been watching me since I walked in.* That was fair; he'd had his eye on the cowboy too.

"Classic. Classier than beer. Dressed to the nines."

Maybe Cowboy had stopped after supper or a meeting.

"Right? You think Juanito is right about his boots?" He winked at Cooper.

"What do I know about cowboy boots, honey?" Coop scoffed. "Juanito isn't exactly Western."

He laughed. "I thought you knew everything about men. Wasn't it you that told me that? Oh my."

How shocked was he when a blond and smiling hottie danced in between them, sights set on Cooper? Far be it from him to come between his friend and a good time. He waved over the guy's shoulder and winked, then made his way off the dance floor.

Oh rats, he'd finished his beer. He'd just have to head back to the bar for another.

The cowboy was still sitting there, strong and silent and

still and sexy as fuck. God, he loved that stoic cowboy thing. Just getting close to that energy made his skin tingle. Made him want to hit his knees.

"Sheila, I lost my dance partner!" He was going to say something to the guy. He didn't know what yet, but something.

"Oh, no! What are you going to do?" Sheila winked at him.

"I'll have what he's having."

"You sure?"

He gaped at her, jaw dropping. "Yes, please, bartender."

Sheila just shook her head at him, laughing. "Coming right up, honey. Sit."

He did sit, one stool over from Cowboy. Despite the way he'd been watched, he was still getting a bit of that arm's length vibe. "Hey. TGIF, huh?"

The cowboy turned to look at him, near-black eyes burning at him like a demon's over sharp cheekbones and a trimmed dark beard. "You know it, honey. Long damn week."

His heart rate sped as he looked into those eyes, and he was thoroughly intimidated. Not scared, not worried, but he definitely had respect. And, Jesus, that voice made his balls ache a little. "Want to talk about it?"

"Nothing much to talk about. Had a good friend and a good man pass away. We put him in the ground today."

"Oh. God, I—I'm so sorry about your friend. He lived in town?"

"Jack and Coke. Enjoy." Sheila winked at him and set it on the bar.

"My treat," the cowboy said, sliding a bill across the bar. "Dave was a local, yeah. We were frat brothers."

"Thank you, sir. UT? Which house?" He picked up the

drink and took a sip, wincing a little at his first taste of the Jack, but mostly it went down pretty well. He looked at the glass. "Not bad."

"Fiji, and yeah, I'm a fifth-generation Longhorn. Hook 'em."

"Hook 'em." He did love football. He held up his glass and took another sip. That one went down better. Fiji. Damn. The guy must have been deep in the closet, or richer than God. Which, okay. Look at the guy's hat. "Fifth-gen? When did you graduate?"

"I got my undergrad in '09, my graduate degree in '11. How about you?" The gravel never left the man's voice, never smoothed out. "I'm straight, by the way."

The cowboy held out one hand.

What? That was impossible. He shook hands with the guy. "Class of 2015. And you have no idea how sorry I am to hear that."

"Pardon?" He got a blink, a single raised eyebrow, and then a grin appeared. "No. No, honey, that's my name. Strait, like King George. Strait McMasters."

"Oh! Oh my God. I'm so sorry." Ordinarily he'd feel like an idiot, but the cowboy—Strait had to get that all the damn time, right? "Tad Dawson. Man, that's a name, huh? Your parents gave you some big shoes to fill."

Class of 2009 made Strait...thirty? Thirty-one? But that voice and the look in those dark eyes...the man came across older.

"Indeed. Daddy's a big fan."

Tad was fascinated by the way Strait's hand wrapped around the glass, brought the whiskey up to his lips. Those lips were pretty interesting too. They definitely had his attention.

"His name doesn't come up often where I'm from in New

Jersey, but I was schooled big-time once I got here. I joke that I stayed for the music, but it's actually pretty true. I love the music scene here." And men like Strait were another reason. Though he couldn't say he'd met anyone quite like this cowboy.

"Yeah, there's nowhere quite like Austin. It's special."

"What are you drinking?" Rory's hand landed on the small of Tad's back, as Rory reached around to grab his glass.

"Jack and Coke." He covered his glass with one hand. "Rory, this is Strait. Strait buried a friend today. I'm keeping him company for a while."

Rory stopped short, stood, and held out one hand. "Man, I'm sorry. That sucks."

"You know it." Strait shook with Rory. "Pleased."

"Rory's another Longhorn, a couple of years before me. 2012? Is that right?"

"You got it. You look a little out of place, Strait. How'd you end up in this bar tonight? Don't seem like your crowd."

"The wake was three doors down. I wanted a drink before I headed home."

"I'm glad you picked this place."

Rory looked at him with one eyebrow raised. "Ah. So, I think I left Juanito alone over there." Rory turned to Strait. "Sorry about your friend. Good to meet you. Safe home."

He winked at Rory and squeezed his friend's hand before Rory headed back toward the dance floor.

Those dark eyes landed on him with an almost physical weight. "Did I piss off your lover?"

He stared into them a second, so infatuated with Strait. Then he blinked and laughed. "No. God, no. He's a fuckbuddy, not a lover. A good one, but just a friend. And he knows me well enough to understand what I meant when I said I was glad you ended up here."

"Yelp said it was friendly, and I'm not looking for a fistfight." Those eyes dragged over his body, making it clear what Strait was looking for.

"Not a fistfight, no. No." He moved over to the empty stool between them and played with the fabric of Strait's dress shirt. "But I'm sometimes...difficult. I like a little convincing."

"Do you now." It didn't sound like a question, not really. Just a statement. "I wouldn't mark that pretty face of yours with a fist."

He shook his head. "I won't consent to that anyway. But..." He reached out and pushed back the cuff of his shirt, letting Strait see the faded marks from last weekend's play.

"Damn, honey, you got you some bruises. I hope it was worth it." Strait traced the marks with one fingertip, sending lightning through his arm.

He wasn't sure how to feel about the light touch over a spot that had been so roughly used just a week ago. It felt good, kind. Not at all like the Dom who had put the marks there. "I got what I needed."

It had been his third time with Bryce. He'd even thought about texting and seeing if the Dom wanted to go for four. Bryce was heavy-handed and rough as hell, but the Dom respected his few rules, played safe, and got him out of his head. He just wished he liked Bryce better. They played well, but they'd never be friends.

He covered Strait's fingers with his other hand and leaned in close. Close enough to allow a kiss. "You've had your eye on me since I walked in."

"I have. You walk like you know how to take it good and hard, and you have a mouth made for sucking."

Mother of God.

Every nerve in his body responded to that: his heart raced, his face flushed hot, and his cock went from interested to...well, fuck. He wasn't sure he could get up and walk right now. He closed the short distance between them like he'd been summoned, pressing his lips to Strait's.

One hand cupped the back of his head, tilting his face and holding him so Strait could take his lips, demanding control of the kiss and fucking his lips like he was storming a beach.

Fuck, yeah. He didn't think he'd ever been kissed like this in a bar before. Or anywhere. Strait's complete focus made him groan, made him want to leave the bar and get naked.

Right. Now.

He let Strait have control for a second, but just long enough to show he was willing before he fought back, tongue shoving and defending. Tad knew he'd lose; he was looking forward to it, but he wanted the cowboy to know he wasn't an easy mark.

Strait chuckled softly into their kiss, those eyes watching him as Strait eased back. "This isn't the place for this, honey."

God, even that laugh sounded like it was running over gravel. He liked it, the sound and the intention both.

"No, Sir." He took a breath and one more sip of his drink, then slid off his barstool. "My place?" He knew his buddies were watching and probably just as stunned as he was. The phone call from Cooper tomorrow would be epic.

"Works for me. I'm parked right outside. You want to ride or follow me?"

He smiled as sweetly as he could manage at Strait. "Can

I trust you with my virtue? No? Good. We can take your car. Mine stays in the garage when I'm drinking."

"Good boy. I had two. I'm good to drive." Strait caught Sheila's gaze and shot her a smile. "Pleased to meet you, ma'am."

Sheila grinned back. "Y'all have a good night. Be good to our boy."

"Night, Sheila. Here comes Coop to get the gossip." He waved to Cooper who gave him two thumbs up and the universal sign for "call me tomorrow", then he hooked his arm through Strait's, and they headed out the door.

2

Good lord and butter, Dave would be tickled as all get out that Strait had picked up a sweet little thing before the dirt had settled on his coffin.

Shit, Dave would have offered to share, and together they would have fucked this doll baby until he didn't remember his own motherfucking name.

"I'm the big black dually over here."

"Of course you are." Tad snorted, running a hand through that short, thick, white-blond hair. "So where do you live that you need this monster?"

"I got a ranch in Bastrop." He really didn't want to explain the ranch, the horses, the boats, all of it. He wanted to have mutual orgasms, maybe quite a few of them.

Tad climbed into the truck, hauling himself up with the oh-shit handle, bicep popping against the long-sleeved shirt. "So, no marks on my face, and I don't do breath play or anything sharp until I know someone well. And I'm not a puppy, a pony, or a latrine. All good?"

Was that even English?

"I don't have a problem, honey." Marks on the face?

Jesus. He'd been known to throw a punch, but not while fucking, as a rule. Possibly ever.

Tad's fingers grazed over his thigh. "We'll get along well, I think. Left at the light, right at the next."

"On it." Strait could remember, when he was a little guy, the east side was fucking scary. Now it was all revitalized and had the best damn food scene.

Tad's hand curled around between his thighs and tucked up nice and snug against his fly. "My building has a garage. Halfway down the block, see the parking sign?"

"I do. You like what you feel?" He was fixin' to turn this boy inside out. His cock ached like nothing going.

"Yes, Sir. I'm definitely impressed." Oh, he could hear the tension in Tad's voice. Very nice.

He wasn't surprised, but it still felt damn fine to hear. He was revved up and loaded for bear. He wanted that touch, skin-on-skin. "You got somewhere you want me to park?"

"Just pull up here, the guys will park it for you." Tad gave one of the attendants a wave as Strait put the truck in park and hopped out to have a conversation. Another guy asked for his keys and handed him a ticket. "See? Easy peasy. Elevator's over there."

"Damn. Look at that." Austin was trying to pretend it was a big city. "Y'all be careful with my girl now."

He loved his truck more than he liked most people.

Tad pressed the button for the elevator and leaned on the wall, looking him over. In better lighting Strait could see that slight frame was more muscular than he thought at first glance, and Tad's eyes were bluer and brighter than the bar lighting made them seem.

Tad smiled as the elevator doors opened. "Going up?"

He let his lips curl. "Or going down. I'll see how it goes."

"I'm all over that." Tad laughed low and hooked fingers

over his belt buckle, pulling him into the elevator and hitting the button for the fourth floor. When the doors closed, Tad dropped right down and mouthed him through his jeans.

Damn, Sam. He ran his fingers through that thick hair, holding Tad where he wanted him for a few seconds before tugging him back so he could look, gauge Tad's arousal.

Tad gasped and looked up at him. Might have been a little of the Jack he was seeing in those bright eyes, but the very obvious ridge pressing against the boy's fly wasn't about booze. That was stone-cold sober need. "Whatever you want. I'm all over it."

The elevator chimed, and Tad straightened up quickly before the doors opened.

Whatever Strait wanted might scare this baby boy away, but he'd take what he could get. "Let's go, honey. What we want needs a sturdy surface and a locked door."

"This way." Tad pulled a key out of a pocket and led him down a long hall, stopping at the last apartment on the floor to open the door. "After you."

The apartment was mostly dark except for some light from the street coming in a window in what he assumed was the living room. Tad followed him in and made a show of loudly turning the lock. "One locked door, Sir."

"Good deal. C'mere." He took his Stetson off with one hand and grabbed Tad and dragged him close with the other.

"Oh." Tad leaned in and smiled up at him, then reached for his hat and hung it just inches away on a hook next to the door. "I'm here. I want the rest of that kiss."

"That can be arranged." He caught Tad by his nape and reeled him right in, reveling in the feel of wanting man pressed all up against him.

"Mmm." The boy wasn't shy, or ashamed, and rubbed right up on his hip. One hand pressed into his chest but the other got friendly, hot palm tucking in right below his buckle.

He wrapped his free hand around Tad's tight little ass and squeezed, jonesing on his sweet handful as he focused on driving them both crazy.

Tad broke away from their kiss suddenly and said, "My safe word is red. Got it? Red. Say it."

"Red." Jesus, safe word? Did this kid have problems? "You sure you want to do this, honey? I ain't a rapist."

Tad blinked at him, then relaxed and smiled coyly. "I know, baby. But what if you wanted to pretend you were? What if you wanted to get rough? How would you know if I'd had enough?" Tad kissed him quickly. "I'm sure I want to do this. Thank you for checking. I thought you liked it when I said I could be difficult." That hand kept rubbing, and Tad never stopped moving, rocking their hips together.

Lord have mercy. Strait just wanted to get their combined rocks off. He took another kiss, this contact meant to leave them both breathless and stupid.

It hit its mark. Tad kissed him back, hungry, and it was a good thing he had an arm around the boy's back when those knees gave out. He turned them, pushing Tad up against the wall to give them a little support. That let him drive them together, finding a quick, rough rhythm to rev them up.

"Fuck! Yes." Tad brought a leg up and hooked it around his ass, and both arms circled up over his shoulders, holding on. "More."

That was more like it. Fuck, this guy was hot as a two-dollar pistol and twice as fine. "Got you. Jeans, honey."

"Yeah. Boots, baby." Tad stepped back to give him room and started pulling off clothing.

He started chuckling and shifted so he could pull his boots off without nutting Tad, because that could be awkward as fuck, not to mention less than sexy.

Tad had stripped bare in the time it took him to get them off and went right to those knees, fingers working his belt open easily. He couldn't make out much more than pale skin in the angular light from the street. The kid got hold of his jeans and tugged them down, sliding them all the way to his ankles so he could step out of them.

Strait unbuttoned his good shirt, shrugging it off, and hanging it on the back of the chair. "This okay here?"

"Uh-huh. Damn. I'm good right here." Tad nuzzled his balls and splayed warm hands out on his thighs for balance.

"You are." He let one hand drop to Tad's head, staring down, loving the visual of his cock, hard and dark, and Tad's paler skin and near-white hair. "Damn, we make a picture."

Tad looked up at him and drew a hot tongue up his length. "Yeah?"

"Yes." He dragged his thumb along Tad's bottom lip, tugging the barest bit to get Tad to open for his prick.

He caught the barest hint of a grin and then Tad's jaw dropped open slowly, the boy's eyes still trained on his.

"No teeth, honey. We clear?" He figured with a mouth like this one had he knew how to use it, but he figured it didn't hurt to make himself crystal clear.

He got a nod, and Tad's tongue darted out, bathing the head of his cock. Oh, that was pretty. Strait did love it when someone worked the tip. Of course, that wasn't common knowledge, even with his lovers.

Tad circled fingers around his shaft and steered him past those soft lips. The boy only went after the head at first with gentle suction and a swirling tongue and then took him deeper, inch by inch, making a promise of things to come.

He hummed softly, offering down a soft bit of praise, even as he began rocking, nice and steady.

Tad let him move and finally took him in deep, holding him there and humming gently before pulling back and taking him in again.

Fucking hell, he'd been right. Tad had a mouth made for sin.

"So good, honey." Hot enough to melt his fucking bones.

It took him a second to understand what Tad was asking by nudging into his hand, but as soon as he threaded his fingers into the boy's hair, everything Tad was doing got more intense. Deeper. Stronger.

Oh, this he got, bone-deep. Strait focused now on moving Tad, fucking the needy lips, tugging the thick hair enough that Tad felt it.

He felt Tad's grunt, and the hungry moan vibrated down into his balls. The kid's tongue scrubbed along his shaft just right, encouraging him in again and again.

A low sound escaped him, and he drove in, tentatively at first, then deeper as Tad didn't complain.

Tad's knees spread wider for balance, and then the boy nodded slightly, made a "hands off" gesture with his hands, then tucked them both behind his back. Just like that, Tad gave over, putting himself, control with Strait.

Oh fucking hell. His balls tightened, and he gritted his teeth. No way was he wasting this. No way in hell.

He cupped the back of Tad's head and started humping in earnest, taking what the sweet baby offered.

He got grunts and the very occasional uncomfortable sound, but Tad didn't once try to pull away, and those hands never left the small of the boy's back. If he paused at all, Tad was hungry, sucking and humming around him.

"Mouth made for sucking." Strait groaned the words,

tightening his grip, his toes curling against the floor.

Tad made a sound almost like a whimper but still let him drive, giving him just the angle, just the pressure he was looking for.

"Fixin' to shoot," he warned. His balls drew up tight, aching. "Take me, and I'll give you what you need, honey."

The boy grunted and quick hands shot out and wrapped around his ass, fingers tugging on him and digging in hard.

He didn't need much, and God knew Tad gave him more than enough. He shot, his eyes crossing, his heart thrumming. Goddamn, that was something else.

"Mmm." He could feel Tad swallow, feel every sweep of that hot tongue as Tad slowly released him. The kid was flushed red, damp bangs stuck to a sweaty forehead, and Tad was panting, fighting for a deep breath.

"Damn." His bones felt like jelly, but he'd be damned if he let on. Jelly legs? Not sexy. "C'mere you."

Tad rocked back on his heels and stood, reaching out for Strait to steady himself. His pupils were big, almost like he was high. "Thank you, Sir."

He hauled Tad up with one hand, bringing them together with an audible slap. "Thank you, honey. I needed that edge off."

Good thing he was good for a twofer, sometimes more.

"My pleasure. Feel good?" Tad went up on tiptoe and kissed him.

Good? Shit. He felt like a million bucks.

He cupped Tad's ass and lifted, rocking them together, letting Tad's body drag against his.

"Oh fuck." Tad gasped at the friction, his own needy erection grinding against Strait's hip. "Please."

"Sweet." He pressed his leg up against Tad's balls, giving him some pressure, a little ache, a tiny burn.

"Yeah." Tad rocked with him, arched against him and that blond head fell back. "'S good, Strait."

"Mmhmm. More?" He didn't wait for an answer; he just pressed in harder, pulled up tighter, giving Tad all the sensation he could.

"Yes, that's...oh! Gonna...oh." He watched Tad's brow wrinkle, swollen lips falling open in a soft gasp. He held the lithe body close when Tad came, the boy trembling against him.

"Mmm... Pretty pretty." He kept Tad right up close, holding tight as he balanced himself.

"Mmm." Tad breathed in deep, and he could feel the boy's smile against his collar bone. "Thank you."

"Anytime, honey. Anytime at all." He nuzzled in, rasping Tad's throat with his chin.

Tad started to laugh. "So, welcome to my place. This is my front hall. Would you like a drink? Maybe a towel?"

"I'd love a glass of water and, yeah, a towel wouldn't go amiss."

"Come on." Tad tugged him down the hall and turned on a light in the bathroom. "Oh man. Bright." Inside they got washcloths and cleaned up and then Tad left him to go get bottles of water.

He hoped Tad was interested in a round two, because he could totally go there. Naked, Tad was even finer than in those skinny jeans.

"Bedroom?" Tad's voice floated down the hall, and he followed the light into the bedroom. A platform bed took up most of the room, and the mattress was covered with a gray faux-suede comforter. That, and the dresser on the far wall with the huge mirror over it made for an interesting space. Contemporary, masculine, and it practically screamed "New Jersey".

It was a far cry from his place, which was all knotty pine and leather accents. His house screamed high-dollar redneck, so it was fair.

"Pretty. It suits you."

"Thanks. Water?" Tad handed him a bottle and then turned the bed down. "I hope you're up for more. I don't think I'm done with you."

"Great minds think alike and all." Strait took the water and drank deep, letting the cold shake the post-orgasm daze off.

"Right on." Tad climbed into bed and patted the thick mattress. "So... Bastrop? Are you a full-time rancher or an 'I live on a ranch' type?"

"I'm retired from my day job, and I have a foreman, so both." He'd developed a new way to drill for natural gas while causing less environmental damage. He'd grown up in the oil industry, and he was tickled shitless that he'd managed to get out now.

"Wait. You're retired? You don't even look thirty-five."

"I turned thirty in February." He was a Valentine's baby.

"You're retired at thirty? Damn. Nice work." Tad snuggled in as he climbed into bed.

He wrapped his arms around Tad and held on, fingers dragging on the smooth, silky skin. "Thank you. What do you do?" *Besides pick up men in bars and blow their minds?*

"Me? I am an expert time-waster. I'm my own boss. I tried the real job thing once, but my father is the worst boss ever." Tad turned and circled a wet tongue around one of his nipples.

"Mine's..." Oh that left a ring of fire that dissolved into an icy, nipple-tightening tingle.

"Hm?" Tad rolled it in his fingers and then went after it

with his tongue again, flicking and teasing, and finally blowing cool air gently across it.

"You're cruising for a bruising," he teased back. Damn, that was maddening as all get out.

"Sounds good to me." Fingers ran over his thigh, around his hip, across his belly.

"Mmhmm." Enough of letting Tad drive. It was his turn. Strait rolled Tad to his back, covering him and drawing one hand up over Tad's head.

"Nice." Tad smiled up at him playfully, then reached up and pinched his other nipple with the free hand, hard enough to sting.

That made him growl, and he grabbed Tad's free hand, gathering them both in one. "Easy."

"Oops?" Tad tugged on against his grip, then tried again. "Damn. Your hands are huge."

"You noticed." He liked a man that paid attention. He leaned down and nibbled Tad's straining upper arm.

"That tickles a little, Sir." Tad twisted under him, but he had the kid pretty well pinned.

He rubbed his chin against Tad's arm, hard enough to buzz, burn a little.

That got a hiss out of the boy and Tad's thigh tucked up behind his balls. "That's...wow."

"Tickle?" He did it again, then repeated it on Tad's nipple.

"Yes. I mean no, not tickle, no. Yes, that feels good." Tad laughed. "Jesus."

"Fair enough." He set to work—nuzzling in, licking, then dragging his teeth over Tad's skin.

He felt Tad's hips lift under him, and the boy's chest rose and fell with a deep, deep breath. Tad tugged again against his grip but didn't seem to be trying to break free.

Strait hummed softly before he bent to one little nipple. He sucked slowly, steadily, knowing that once he got it nice and swollen, his beard would sting so good.

"Mmm. Yeah." Tad arched to his mouth with a gorgeous sigh.

Slow and steady, he sucked, bringing the blood up to the surface. Every so often he flicked the tip of that hard nip with his tongue.

"Strait." Tad twisted and rocked to one side, trying to move beyond the reach of his tongue, trying to frustrate him.

He bit down on the tight nipple—not hurting, but a clear warning.

Tad's little whimper was lovely, and strangely delicate for someone who claimed they liked a fight. The boy relaxed, arms going slack, chest sinking with a deep sigh.

"There you go." He went back to his good work, focusing on making one little nipple scream with pleasure before moving to the second.

Tad moaned and arched to his lips, graceful as a dancer. So damn pretty. Strait could watch Tad move for days.

He lifted his head and blew a long, slow stream of air over Tad's swollen flesh, and Tad gasped, tugging on those hands again. "I want to touch you."

There was no play in that statement at all. Tad's voice was low and heated, half-lidded eyes focused on him.

"Mmm..." There was nothing wrong with that. "Such a pretty boy."

He let Tad's wrists go, bringing one hand down to kiss.

Tad smiled at the gesture, watching him. "Such a handsome gentleman." Warm fingers tugged lightly on his beard, pulling him down into a kiss.

His lips felt swollen and hot as they kissed, both of them

moaning. Tad's fingers slid into his hair, and one hand continued down over his back.

Damn, that touch made his eyes cross, and he pushed down against Tad, rubbing hard.

Tad's knees drew up to hug his hips, offering. "Nightstand. Lower drawer."

That was straightforward as fuck. He approved. It didn't mean he wasn't going to tease some, but he totally approved.

He reached down, finding lube and condoms in the drawer. Strait slicked up his fingers, tracing a lazy circle around that tiny ring of muscles.

Curious fingers found a nipple, teasing and testing it as Tad rolled to meet his touch. "You've got soft hands for a big guy."

"I have a great manicurist." He was joking, but it sounded way classier than *I have dry skin, even in Austin*.

"Oh, bullshit." Tad laughed and pinched his nipple lightly. "You're a fucking cowboy."

"I am. With stock in coconut oil." He pressed the tip of his finger into Tad just up to the first knuckle.

"Handy." Tad exhaled heavily and arched, trying to take in more.

"You know it." He backed off with a hum, waiting for Tad to breathe, relax, let him drive.

That earned him a frustrated grunt. "What...what. Where'd you go?"

"Breathe, baby. I will give you what you need." He was good at that.

He pressed back in, tapping Tad's hole before stretching it.

"Yes, Sir." Tad took a deep breath and exhaled, relaxing visibly, just as if he'd given the kid an order.

"There we go." He began to fingerfuck Tad, nice and slow, steady. He was going to make Tad feel so damn good.

Tad sighed, fingers gliding lightly over his chest. Tad was on fire when the kid was all wound up but getting Tad to relax was something else. The boy was light but not fragile, sweet but hungry for him.

He groaned softly, bending to nibble on Tad's shoulder, and he pressed deeper.

"Mmm." Tad hummed in his ear, hands running down his back, up his sides. "I'm not very patient, you know."

"No? Patience is a virtue, I hear." He managed to say the words without even a smile.

"I'm not very virtuous either. Oh...god." He felt Tad tighten around his finger, the movement probably reflex.

"Good spot, hmm?" Strait chuckled and repeated the touch, once, twice, three times.

That made Tad gasp, his back slowly bending in a shameless and graceful arch as he bore down against Strait's hand. "Fuck."

"Yeah. Damn, baby, you're so pretty." Strait added a little more slick, then slid in a second and third finger in short order.

He had Tad moaning, tight ass taking whatever he dished out, hips rocking to meet his intrusion. The boy's body was begging, but Tad wasn't. Yet.

Luckily patience was Strait's virtue, all the way, so he could wait.

He pressed in, stroking Tad inside, spreading him wide.

Tad groaned and dropped a hand down to stroke himself, eyes full of need burning into Strait's.

"Mmm..." The urge to growl that was his? Christ, that was huge. Ridiculous, but huge.

"Fuck, yeah." Tad arched up, nibbled his ear and whispered, "Deeper, cowboy. Let me have you."

"Gonna give you my cock soon, fuck you 'til neither one of us can see." He pushed in hard, finger-fucking Tad with intent.

Tad gasped and nodded. "Please, Sir. Yes, please."

"Pretty baby." He gloved up and slicked his prick with one hand, trying his damnedest to keep Tad all nice and revved up at the same time.

Tad was watching him. The kid rocked into his hand. "Gonna be so good. Want it. Want you."

"You're fixin' to have me." Strait eased his slick fingers out, replacing them with his cock.

The kid let him in, let him touch himself deep, fingers working over his shoulders and digging in trying to find a spot to hold on. "You feel good."

"That is no lie." He groaned, panting a little bit to keep from just bashing into that tight little hole, over and over.

Fingers wrapped around the back of his neck, and Tad grinned at him as everything went tight around his shaft. "You're not going to hurt me, cowboy."

"Thank fuck." He pulled out almost all the way, and then he slammed in, the pleasure climbing his spine.

The sound Tad made was loud and needy, and the kid's whole body moved under him, with him, that hard prick rubbing against his belly.

Fuck yes. He groaned and went to town, sawing in and out, driving into Tad, watching for a hint that the sweet boy needed him to stop.

He didn't get one, not for a long while. Not until the two of them were breathless and Tad was flushed and sweating. "Please." The boy's voice was hoarse and dry. "Please, I need to—can I—oh, god."

"Come on, baby. Come for me." Strait managed to balance and get one hand wrapped around Tad's prick.

That touch was just about all it took. Tad rocked under him and shot, body trembling against his, lungs gulping air.

"Good boy." Damn, that was—his eyes crossed, and he gave Tad a few wild strokes before he lost it, filling the condom with a grunt.

Tad pulled him down and kissed him, clinging to him, keeping them close. "Thank you, Sir."

"Oh, you're more than welcome. That was fine as frog hair." He took another kiss, and then another. "Damn."

"Damn. Yeah." Tad laughed gently, still catching his breath, fingers holding on tight. "I'm boneless."

"You're hot as the hinges of hell, baby." And he meant that.

"Well, you're inspiring. Just what I needed." Gentle fingers played with his beard, stroked over his cheek. "Are you staying?"

"You inviting me, baby, because I'd love to." He could enjoy a few more sessions before he offered to take Tad to breakfast.

Tad smiled and pulled him down onto his side. "I'm inviting you."

"Mmm..." Strait settled, both of them shifting until they found where they fit together. "This cool, baby?"

"Mmhmm. You're comfy. Nap?" The kid nuzzled right in.

"Hell yeah." He kissed the top of Tad's head. "Holler when you're ready for round two."

"Three. And you'll know." He got a sleepy chuckle and then Tad went quiet.

Damn, he'd hit the jackpot. Dave would be tickled as shit. Orgasms were a great way to honor a brother, after all.

3

---

*There's a cowboy in my bed this morn*ing, Tad texted Cooper and then hit start on the coffee maker.

Still.

He'd taken a number of cowboys home, but unless the man in question was hammered, they always went home when he asked if they'd like to stay.

He'd known from the minute Strait's dark eyes met his that this one was different. He'd never met a man who could make him want like that with a look. He'd let a lot of men think they could, that was part of the pick-up game, but this cowboy had earned it.

Sorry, honey. Is he hungover? Just kick him out.

He grinned at Cooper's text. *Nope. He's just good for four rounds.* Really good.

O.O jealous. Juanito fell asleep when I got him home.

Four rounds, not a one the same as the one before, and he was sore as hell. His ass was worn out. His ass, his back, his thighs, his shoulders...he'd been well used—and well looked after too. He felt fantastic.

What's his story? Rory said he was coming from a funeral?

Yeah. Long story. Call me later?

Sure. Going back to bed?

You know it. He was going to bring the cowboy some coffee and then see where things went from there.

He fixed up two cups and headed into the bedroom. Strait was solid and dark, muscled and fuzzy, stretched out on his bed. He was sporting a morning hard-on, the thick, proud prick curving up over his belly.

The sight took his breath away and he stopped in the doorway for a second to just take the man in. Fuck, he was a lucky bastard.

"Good morning." The greeting sounded more suggestive than he'd intended; his voice was raw, and his throat felt dry. *Too much screaming and swallowing cock*, he thought smugly. He'd take it.

"Mmm...mornin'." Jesus, he'd thought Strait's voice was deep and low last night. This smile, though, it was lazy and knowing and admiring and happy to see him. It made him feel warm.

"I brought you coffee. I didn't know how you took it, so I guessed at just a little milk." He smiled back. Preferring naked over clothed any day, he hadn't dressed to make coffee, so he set both mugs down on the nightstand next to Strait and climbed over the cowboy to get back in bed.

One warm hand ghosted over his ass as he moved, the caress making his skin tingle.

"You look pretty happy, cowboy." Which was a big improvement over the man that was staring into a Jack and Coke after his friend's funeral.

"You're something to wake up to, baby." Strait sipped the coffee, and then he took a big gulp. "Good shit."

"Thanks. I'm not picky about much, but I'm picky about my coffee." He was picky about men, too. Men he wanted anyway. He had a type for sure, and Strait checked all the boxes.

"I hear that. Good coffee, good whiskey, good company."

"Cheers to that." He touched his mug to Strait's. "Are you hungry? A big guy like you must need some calories, huh? You want me to make something for breakfast?"

"I could eat, or I could take you out. I'm easy, baby." Those dark eyes twinkled out at him.

Take him out? Like, be seen with him in public? Maybe Strait was still drunk. Or hungover. "Can we please go out?"

"Totally. Where do you want to go?" That was immediate, relaxed, and easy.

"Eastside Cafe. Ever been there? It's great." He could go for the migas.

"I haven't, but I'm in." Strait rubbed a line along his belly, down to his hip. "Mmm...that's a nice touch right there."

Yeah, it was. "I like it." He set his coffee down and leaned into Strait, close enough for a kiss if Strait wanted one, and drew his fingers up one of the cowboy's thighs.

"Hey, baby." Strait scooped him up, kissing him with focus, hands curled around his ass.

He pushed his fingers into Strait's dark hair and tangled them there, holding on.

Jesus. Strait's kiss made him wanton. Made him willing to give up whatever Strait wanted. His body, his time, his obedience...anything. And it was just a kiss. What he'd have been willing to give over last night went much deeper.

Strait eased him over onto his lap, the heat from the strong body pushing through his skin, into his muscles.

"Mmm." He stretched up tall, straddling thick thighs, showing off a little for the cowboy. When he sat back down, nice and close, he made sure his cock pressed up against Strait's. "You're a sight, Mister."

"Mmm. You're warm." Strait's eyelids went heavy and low, and the strong hands landed on his ass.

"I tend to run hot." Damn, look at those eyes. If he could do that, he wanted to see what else he could do. He slid fingers under Strait's balls and stroked the skin there, hard enough not to just be teasing.

"Uhn." Those fingers dug into his ass, squeezing hard. "Damn, baby."

He moved his fingers, circling them around Strait's cock and his own, squeezing them together. The pressure and the heat were sweet, though his hand wasn't quite big enough for both of them. "Haven't had enough of me yet?"

"Not even close." That was sure, clear, and just a little overwhelming.

Well, okay then. Brunch was becoming lunch. Or maybe linner. Lupper?

Fuck, who cares? There's a cowboy in your bed during daylight.

God, he loved the little devil on his shoulder.

He bent and went after Strait's nipple with his teeth, only pinching lightly, letting the threat dangle out there.

"Mmm... Are you hungry?" Strait didn't sound near worried enough.

"Uh-huh. Are you?" He licked the spot, bathing it and all the soft fuzz around it with his tongue and then sucked it into his mouth hard enough to bruise if he could keep it up long enough.

"Starving. Damn, baby!" Strait sounded so turned on, so shocked.

He didn't go for the bruise; the reaction was enough. He

released Strait, laughing softly, one lazy hand stroking Strait's erection. "You like that?"

"Nope. Not a bit." Okay, that little curled lip, the grin—that was sexy as fuck. "You sure do trip my trigger, baby."

"I do, huh?" He smiled at Strait. That might go down as one of the sexiest things anyone had ever said to him. Where did this guy come from? Maybe Strait's friend was now a guardian angel. "I'd say you've got my number too, cowboy."

He went in for another one of those kisses he couldn't get enough of and whispered against Strait's lips. "I don't know how you can be so hungry when you've been feasting all night."

"It's the best sort of addiction. There's so much to explore." Strait never looked away from him, those dark eyes burning into him.

He couldn't remember the last time someone looked at him and wanted to...*see* him. And no one had ever looked at him like that for sure. He didn't understand what was happening in the rancher's head, but something was.

They were both turned on, but no one was rushing; he was enjoying this space where they could, but they didn't, and he thought maybe Strait was too. He did his best to hold Strait's gaze, even when it got uncomfortable, even when he thought maybe Strait was seeing more than he wanted anyone to.

Strait made a low, happy sound before reaching up and stroking his jaw, the act breathtakingly intimate.

He inhaled sharply at the touch, felt his cheeks heat, and thought maybe he was having a heart attack. Or a stroke. Or some not-breathing...thing. "I... I don't understand what you're doing."

"Learning about you. Like you're learning about me." There was real kindness in Strait's gaze, but not worry.

"Okay." Strait wanted to learn about him. And it wasn't a weird stalker thing, it was genuine. Or it seemed genuine. Tad thought maybe he'd like it to be.

Maybe. God. He hadn't thought that they were learning things; he thought he was just having fun.

"But I get the feeling there's a whole lot for me to learn."

"Not hardly. I'm just a dude." Strait grinned at him. "Simple and straightforward."

"Uh-huh. Right." Yeah...not so much. There was something about Strait that wasn't simple at all, something complex under the man's skin and behind those dark eyes. Strait might be just a dude at a bar, but not in the bedroom.

He smiled, keeping his tone light. "Simple, straightforward guys don't look at me like that. Straightforward guys give me a smack on the ass, thank me for the nightcap, and get a Lyft back to their apartment. Simple guys don't stay the night."

Only the interesting guys did that. The ones he had to think about a little more.

"Oh you're so much more fascinating than that. I could spend a couple three weeks on your smile."

Whoa. That was just an expression, right? "Talking weeks already, huh? Maybe we should see if we can make it through breakfast first." Anyway, his smile couldn't be that interesting.

"Fair enough. I'm all over making it through breakfast. Can I get migas or pancakes where we're going?"

"Both, but the migas are outstanding. It's already ordered in my head." He leaned in and rested their foreheads together. "You're obviously a guy that knows what he wants. That's hot as hell, in case you're interested. I didn't mean to turn a hose on this."

He felt like Strait had leapt ahead of him by a mile, and he was half blind and on crutches and trying to catch up.

"I tend to be, yeah. I'm bossy, or so I've been told." Strait rubbed their noses together, the connection sweet as fuck.

"I like it. Stay bossy." He dared a quick kiss, skin starting to tingle remembering how Strait had taken charge at all the right moments last night. "Tell me what to do. Tell me what you want. I'll do it."

"Mmm...listen to you. I approve." Strait took his hand and wrapped it around Strait's heavy cock, which was flagging, but still impressive in his fingers. "Touch me, baby."

"Thank you, Sir. I'd love to." He tightened his grip and stroked a couple of times, encouraging it to stretch and stiffen, palming the head every few strokes to help it along. "I'm a fan."

"Mmm..." Strait leaned back, eyes down on Tad's hand. "You have good hands. Seriously, baby."

He loved how Strait was watching, and Tad let the touch intensify, a little harder, a little faster, more pressure. He hissed and hummed for Strait, hot sounds, appreciating how real and truthful the whole thing was.

Strait's hand found his cock, and that touch began to move, to copy his motions, so that in this trippy way, he was jacking himself through Strait.

He grinned at first, like he might laugh, but Strait got something just right, and he moaned instead. "That's...oh, man. So weird. And—" Tad couldn't manage to finish his thought. He pumped Strait harder and dropped his eyes down to watch too.

"Uh-huh. It's fucking wild right?" Strait grinned, the

look heavy-lidded and wondering.

Strait's eyes said things he couldn't quite read, but he really wished he could. "Wild." He tried not to rock up into Strat's hand, but paying attention was becoming a little difficult. "So...wild."

"Uh-huh. Let yourself go, baby. Feel it." God, Strait said the sweetest things.

"Yes, Sir." That was an order he could live with. He let himself move, taking Strait along with him, fingers still curled tight.

The wickedness in this game made itself known when he lost focus, and the rhythm of both their hands slowed.

"Shit." He laughed gently and blinked his vision clear. "Oh. I have to...like you're me, huh? God. Okay."

"You got it. You've got me in the palm of your hand." Strait had laser-focus, and it was directed at him.

"Yes, Sir." He looked down again, the sight of their hands on each other enough to make his cock twitch in Strait's fingers. He pushed his thumb through the slit of Strait's prick and moaned as Strait did the same. "Fuck that's hot."

"You got that shit right. Do it again."

He glanced up at Strait just to see if the intensity in the man's face matched what was in that voice, and damn, did it ever. He did as he was told, gliding his thumb through and adding a little pressure. Strait's answering move was enough to make him gasp.

They worked together, Strait following his lead like a dream, every stroke making him ache. Finally Tad closed his eyes so he wouldn't be distracted and let his hand fly, every move meant to drive them higher, closer. Strait was amazing, irresistible, making him crazy. "Yeah...close." God, he sounded hoarse.

"Beautiful baby. More. Come on." Strait still sounded

smooth as glass.

Fuck. He knew Strait was a mile behind him and forced a deep breath, focusing on Strait's silky prick. He gave the cowboy more, but as soon as he did, Strait did the same, making his eyes cross and his concentration dissolve. "Fuck. I —sorry, Sir. I can't... I need..." Jesus he didn't even know what he was saying. His hand sped and he pushed up into Strait's fist.

"There we go. Come on, baby. More." Strait started jacking him with a steady stroke, the touch meant to get him off.

He hovered on the edge for what seemed like forever— close to agony, or nirvana, or maybe dying. Then everything shorted out on him all of a sudden and he baptized them both in hot spunk.

"I got you, baby." Strait's touch had moved to cradling his balls, holding them in one hot hand.

He heard that but he didn't answer, mostly because he wasn't sure he was breathing. He got a gulp of air and that was good, and if he blinked enough he could actually see things. He dropped his head forward onto Strait's shoulder.

"Holy fucking shit." He was relieved that he could speak through all the panting.

"I hear that. You did so good, baby."

"I did?" Oh, that felt so good to hear. He didn't know what he'd done, but the praise just lifted him right up. He picked his head up and found a smile for Strait so Strait would know. "Thank you, Sir."

"Thank you." Strait took a soft, lazy kiss. "That was fun as all get out."

Mmm. Kisses. "Did you...?" He looked down between them. "Do you want me? Let me suck you off." He pushed back, eyes on Strait's gorgeous cock.

"I want you, baby. Get me off, and I'll take you out for food." Strait pushed at the base of his cock, making a clear offer.

Food eventually. Right now he had a feast in front of him. He shifted low, stretching out on his stomach. He didn't tease, but he took one lazy taste, running his tongue around the head and through the salty slit before taking Strait fully into his mouth.

"Fuck yeah." Strait arched up, proving how bad the man needed his mouth, right now.

Right on. He loved this, and he knew he was good at it. He hummed approval, slid an encouraging hand under Strait's ass, and took Strait as deep as he could manage.

Praise poured down on him, Strait not holding anything back. He soaked it in and gave Strait everything he wanted, swallowing hard when he could, giving Strait pressure and heat.

"Fixin' to, baby. Close." Such a polite cowboy.

Bring it, he wanted to say. Instead, he caught Strait's prick by the base and steered it into his throat.

Strait bucked into his mouth and shot, barking out a wild fucking cry.

He got a tingle up his spine, loving being able to make Strait lose it a little. "Mmm." Tad hummed and licked and soothed Strait's spent prick, enjoying the calm after the storm.

"Goddamn, that was fine." Strait blinked down at him, dark eyes unfocused.

Strait was the hottest thing on earth looking at him that way. It made him feel like he could burst, he was so...happy. "Thank you, Sir." He sat up and straddled the cowboy again, leaning down for a kiss.

Strait groaned, this kiss lazy, sloppy, satisfied. One hand was in his hair, thumb rubbing his neck.

"That was amazing." He kissed Strait again, liking the lazy, sweet connection. "You're amazing."

"You tripped my trigger, honey. All of them." Strait offered him the sweetest grin. "Once I have bones again, I'll feed us."

"I need a quick shower. Then you can feed me." He smiled. "You're welcome to take one too." He wiggled back and slid off the bed.

"Is it big enough for two?" Strait stood and stretched, the heavy muscles fascinating with how they moved and rippled.

God he could just stand here and look. Except he wanted Strait to talk too because the way the cowboy called him "baby" made him feel a little dizzy. "Come on."

His bathroom was pretty good sized considering and his shower was big enough for two normal-sized people, so it was a good thing he was on the trim side because Strait took up a lot of space. He loved it.

Strait took the soap up and began to wash him, exploring his body like he had all the rights to do it. The touches weren't even sexual, more curious, learning.

He just watched Strait's face, the eyes so focused on him, the deliberate way Strait moved, fingers that touched him like he meant something. It was hard to believe it was really happening. Whatever "it" was.

Strait turned him toward the tile and began working his back and shoulders, fingers digging in and turning the cleansing into a deep massage.

He braced his hands on the shower wall and sighed, leaning into the massage. "You can't be real."

"No? I'm feeling pretty damn real right now." Strait nuzzled his nape.

"Jesus, you feel real. You sure fuck like you're real. But this is totally a dream." And he was having a really hard time waking up. He had no idea what to do with Strait... Tad was ready to do anything the cowboy wanted.

"You have to be anywhere today, sweet baby?"

"No, Sir." Not until the club later, but if Strait...

"Then you and me can just dream together, yeah? I'm all over that." Strait worked the big muscles of his glutes, and the release damn near killed him.

He nodded, because when he opened his mouth to answer all that came out was a moan. *Me too. All damn day if you want me.* He felt like he was being spoiled. Pampered. Worshipped. Wasn't that his job? He'd never expected a guy to...not for him.

"Oh, right there. I got you, baby. You got some tension here." Strait hummed and drew circles on the small of his back.

"Owowow...whoa." That was one of those hurts so good things. "You don't have to...oh, but please don't stop."

"No stopping. Breathe, huh?" That beard rasped against his shoulder.

"Breathing." He took a breath and tried to exhale the tension away. Breathing was a good idea, he felt much less light-headed. Duh.

"Good." To his shock, Strait bent down and soaped his legs, then his feet. God, how intimate was that?

He tried not to mess with the mood, but he giggled because his toes were ticklish. "Easy, cowboy."

"Ticklish? Good to know." Strait stood and stretched tall under the spray.

Oh. His turn. He turned around and ran his hands from

Strait's belly all the way up to the cowboy's broad shoulders, watching the way his fingers moved over the landscape of muscle and through the fuzzy hair at Strait's sternum.

He grabbed the soap and started washing, though he couldn't quite reach well enough everywhere. They ended up laughing about it, and Strait took the soap from him.

The rest of the shower was quick, Strait taking a fraction of the time cleaning himself before rinsing them both off. "I'm starving, baby. You're one hell of a workout."

"Ha. Me too. Who needs the gym with you around?" He winked, flirting as they dried off. "Migas are calling me."

"Are they? We'd better get to it, then. You have a clean toothbrush by any chance?"

He laughed and opened the cabinet under the sink, grabbing a brand-new hot pink toothbrush. "Here you go. So butch."

"I am secure in my masculinity, baby. Pink looks damn fine on me."

Laughing harder, he grabbed his electric toothbrush, and handed the toothpaste to Strait. They brushed and bumped elbows and shared the sink like he and his college roommates used to, only this was...fun. Oddly, it made him happy.

Dressing was a quick business, and they were heading out in no time. Tad dug up sunglasses and a ballcap and handed Strait his hat.

"Thank you. Let's go get us some migas." Strait shot him a straight-up pirate smile. "Then we'll see what wickedness we can get up to."

Somehow he didn't think it was going to be too difficult for the two of them to get into something wicked. All they really needed was privacy.

And possibly not even that.

4

Good lord and butter, Strait was about stuffed as a tick. They'd eaten and had a couple of mimosas, driven over to Town Lake for a walk, and sure as shit, they had found a food cart with kolaches and had shared one.

Now he wanted to get home, get in the pool, and cook a couple steaks for supper.

He just had to convince Tad to come on.

"Have a great day." Tad stepped back from the shepherd he'd been petting and smiled at Strait. "What a gorgeous day. Perfect day for walking a dog. I wish I could have a dog, but I'm terminally negligent when it comes to pets. Cooper has talked me out of getting one a bunch of times."

Tad had stopped to pet every dog that walked by. One thing he had to say; the kid was friendly.

"I have three Great Pyrenees, at least right now." Marge was due to have her third litter in the next week. He thought, especially if she threw a good little bitch, that it would be her last. Marge was a great momma, and she deserved to live the rest of her life on the ranch in peace.

"Oh, so pretty. And big. Wow. But I guess with the ranch

and everything they have room to roam." Tad found them a bench and took a seat.

"They do. I got a decent-sized spread." Strait settled next to Tad. "I won a place that burned in the big fire in a poker game. I've been working on it ever since."

"Wow. Doing the work yourself? I'm impressed. I'm pretty useless with a hammer." Tad grinned at him. "I'm really good with opening beer for hardworking cowboys though."

"I wish I could say I did it all myself, baby. Truth is, I got me a great contractor, a ranch foreman, and one hell of a staff. I do like to help out, though, and I did the pool house on my own." And it looked fucking amazing, if he said so himself.

"Helping out counts. I'd still bring the guy that paid for hardworking people a beer. I'm just going to hang onto the image of you putting up a fence on a super-hot day for a while." Tad hummed at him.

"You want to come out and see it? Have a swim?" The words were out of his mouth before he even really thought, but he meant it. He wanted to show off his ranch, his home to Tad.

He watched an entire debate flash by in the kid's blue eyes. He wasn't sure what he was expecting Tad to say exactly, but he liked the look.

"You have a pool?" Tad's eyes were wide, and he sat forward on the bench. "I mean...sorry. You're inviting me out? You don't have to do that, it's cool. But I appreciate the thought."

"I am. I have a pool, a hot tub. I'd love for you to come." He let his grin go naughty, wicked. "I'd love to watch you swim."

Tad returned his grin with an equally suggestive look.

"I'm an excellent swimmer. I was on the diving roster at UT."

"No shit? Wow. That rocks, baby. Now I need to see you. You want to stop and get some clothes? We can go play." It was important to him, somehow, that Tad said yes.

Tad stared at him like his eyes were going to tell the kid something his mouth hadn't already said and then nodded. "Okay. Yes. I'd love to."

"Fuckin' A. You okay with me driving? I can bring you home tomorrow, no problem." Lord have mercy, what was he doing? Why did it feel so good?

"That's fine, I don't have plans. I would like to grab a few things at my place if that's okay." Tad stood again and backed away slowly, smiling at him, mischief in those bright eyes. "Do you have a diving board?"

"I do, yeah." He couldn't do anything fancy-assed, but he preferred the full-body shock for his morning swim rather than wading in and doing it inch by inch.

"I can't wait." Tad turned away, giving him a good look at the kid's backside in strategically faded jeans.

Sweet baby. Strait wanted to just eat him up.

Again.

Strait stood and stretched, before he caught up with Tad, daring to stroke one finger against his wrist.

Tad inhaled sharply and let the breath out on a sigh. "Goose bumps."

"That's a good thing. At least I think so."

"Yeah." Tad nodded, and he was pretty sure the color in the kid's cheeks was a blush, not the sunshine. "I think so too."

"Come on. Let's go pick up your things, stop at Sonic, and head to the ranch."

"Mmm. Hell yeah. Asian sweet chili wings and a frozen

grape limeade." Tad skipped ahead—literally skipped—headed for the truck.

"Weirdo." Everyone knew it was a footlong coney and a cherry limeade.

"Weirdo? What? It's not like I'm ordering a cherry limeade." Tad bounced next to the driver's side door, waiting for him.

He cracked up, clicking the door locks. "I may order two."

"Oh, not you too? It's Cooper's favorite. Cherry. Gross." Tad jogged around and hopped in. "The kolaches were so good weren't they? God, I'm hungry though. Good call."

Hadn't he just been thinking how stuffed he was? And Tad was hungry.

It didn't surprise him, though. He reckoned Tad was the Energizer Bunny, going a million miles a minute. That had to come from somewhere.

"What's on the radio, cowboy? Can I listen?" Tad reached for his radio with quick fingers, turning it on.

"Whatever you like, but I get a veto. Fair?"

"Yes, Sir. You're in charge. Plus it's your truck." Tad cycled through the stations, pausing on one for a second and then moving on to the next and the next. Just when he was about to veto Tad's ability to search at all, the kid settled on Bob Marley.

That worked. It wasn't Kenny Chesney, but it so worked.

"Man, you have a stereo system in here."

"I do." He had stereo systems everywhere. He was a music fiend.

"So what's your jam? Garth? McGraw?"

"Like them both. Love Maroon Five, the Beatles, Queen. I like music." He loved it loud when he felt like he was rattling around in the house.

"Cool. Nice." Tad kicked his shoes off, reclined the seat back a little, and put his feet up on the dash. "I like pretty much everything too. It's a good thing I don't have a roommate, nobody wants to hear me singing along with Maren Morris and Carrie Underwood."

"You should hear me try to rap." He shot Tad a grin. "It's a sad thing."

"Ohhh...shit." Tad shot him a mock-horrified look and started giggling, totally off the deep end.

He flicked Tad's thigh, but he laughed along. "It's a tough job, but someone has to do it."

"No shit. Try hitting some of those notes with Carrie. I sound like a goose being strangled." Tad plucked his sunglasses from the cup holder and put them on.

"I can't wait to hear." He had a great karaoke set up from his twenty-fifth birthday party. He'd have to get Mitch to find it.

"Yeah, okay. If you rap first."

They stopped by Tad's place so he could grab some stuff, but he was in and out almost before Strait noticed he was gone. That was gratifyingly eager.

Tad sat up as they pulled into Sonic, stomach growling loudly. "Oh man. Can I add some tater tots too, please, Sir? I'm starving."

"Anything you want, baby." He was easy. He might go for an order of chili cheese tots himself. By the time they ordered, they had three bags, plus Route 44 drinks. Damn.

Tad opened one of the bags and dug into the chicken. "Oh. Yeah. So yummy. What do you want first?"

"Hmm. Grab me a mozzarella stick?" He did love him some fried cheese.

"Mozzarella...got it." Tad pulled one out of the bag and held it to his lips, grinning. "Open wide."

He opened up, snapping the bite in half. Yum. Cheesy goodness.

"Ha! Watch my delicate fingers." Tad laughed, looking happy and relaxed, and ate the other half of his cheese stick. "Oh. That's good."

The drive went by pretty quickly, with Tad eating and feeding him bites as he drove. The kid spent a lot of time checking out the scenery, but every now and then Tad would look over at him and just smile or rest a hand on his arm or his knee, just as sweet as could be.

He pulled onto his road, eyes checking the fences automatically. They looked good from here—solid, sturdy, strong. The guys were doing a damn fine job.

"We must be close. We're in the middle of nowhere. Cowboys always live in the middle of nowhere." Tad sat up and started cleaning up the wrappers and napkins all over the cab of his truck.

"We're fixin' to get to my driveway. This is the S-Bar-M ranch on both sides. The house is up on the left."

"Well, Mr. S-Bar-M, it sure looks big. I'm not the least bit surprised." Tad's straw made a loud slurping sound as he finished the last of the grape concoction he was drinking.

"I'm proud of it." It had taken up a huge part of his recent life—maybe all of it—and it was one of the best things he'd ever created.

Tad took off his seatbelt and leaned over the center console to kiss his cheek. "I can't wait to see it all." The kid sounded a hundred percent sincere.

"Thanks, baby. I want to show off to you." Hell, he wanted Tad to meet his dogs.

"Oh... Strait. Look at your house!" Tad practically hopped in his lap despite the steering wheel.

The ranch house was vast, with three wings, cut stone

walls, and a huge wraparound porch. You couldn't see the pool area from here, because it was hidden in the back, but the copse of pecan trees framed the whole thing, and he could see them.

He pulled around the driveway, parking the truck right at the front door. One of the guys would move it in a bit.

"Ta-da! The old homestead."

"Homestead. Jesus Christ. It's enormous!" Tad hopped out of the truck and ran around to his side. "It's gorgeous. Wow. Remind me never to play poker with you. Damn."

"Let me grab your bag, and I'll give you the tour." He wanted to show off a little and then get Tad in the pool.

Tad blinked at him as he shouldered the duffel. "Thank you, Sir."

"You're welcome, baby. Come on in." He leaned down, kissed Tad good and hard.

Damn, there was something about this guy. He figured it was because he'd lost Dave, but it didn't matter, did it?

They were having a good time.

Tad leaned into him, swaying a little as he pulled away. "Come in. Sure. Yes, Sir." Blue eyes blinked at him.

"Are you pretty or what?" He had to smile, because this man did it for him.

"Oh, stop. Show me your house." Tad took his arm, and leaned against him, pushing him toward the front door.

Strait laughed and hit his keypad entry, No one hardly ever came through the grand entrance, but Tad deserved to see it. The foyer was warm—stone and wood everywhere. The view straight ahead was all windows, highlighting the outdoor kitchen and living area with the pool.

Tad walked in, looking around like he was in a museum. He peeked into the rooms off the foyer and then headed back to the windows, taking in the view.

Strait started to wonder whether he should worry because Tad—the guy who never stopped talking—was completely silent for a bit. But as soon as he joined Tad at the windows, Tad took his hand and tangled their fingers.

"It's amazing, Strait. Just...it's perfect. I love it. What a beautiful place."

"Thank you. Seriously." He'd put his soul into making this a sanctuary, a safe space.

"I can't wait to get in that pool. You really live in this big place all alone?" Tad wandered back up the hall.

Ah, the chatterbox was back. That must be a good sign.

"I do. The left wing is bedrooms, the center wing is the kitchen and dining area, and the right wing is the media room, the office, and the gym."

"My dad has all of those things in his wing too. So adult." Tad chuckled and grinned at him. "In my apartment, they're all the same room. Did I even show you that room?"

"We were busy. Really busy." He winked back. "You can do it next time."

"So busy." Tad laughed. "Where do I put on my suit?"

"You have options. You can come see my bedroom or there's the pool house." Either way worked. He had a great view regardless.

"Well, where are you changing? You think we should save the bedroom for when we're ready to get busy again later?" Tad flirted with him, placing hands on his chest.

"We can go out to the pool house. I have a suit in there." If he needed to wear it.

"Works for me. Lead the way, I brought my diving suit."

He led Tad through the great room and into the kitchen. "This is the easiest way out to the back."

He opened the big French doors and led Tad to the edge of the pool.

"Wow. Nice. I can't wait to get in. This place is so great." Tad followed him into the pool house and wasted no time putting on the smallest bathing suit he'd ever seen. It was almost obscene, it was so small.

"Pretty," he muttered. He grabbed a pair of trunks and sat to pull off his boots and jeans.

"Thank you. Can't dive with everything loose, you know? Ow." Tad pulled two towels off a shelf by the door and handed him one before running back to the edge of the pool. "Gonna check the water. God, I haven't been in the pool in forever."

"Yeah, that's the downside to living in a high rise than a normal complex, isn't it?" He'd lived in a complex in Houston for a while that had a lovely pool area. Too bad it wasn't private.

Tad dipped his toes in and smiled. "Not cold." He headed straight for the diving board and tested out the spring. "How deep is the pool? Nine feet? Twelve? Don't want to crack my head open."

"It's a twelve down at that end." He climbed in at the shallow end and sat on the steps so he could admire.

"Awesome. Don't judge, I need to get a feel for the board." He watched as Tad bounced three times, using the last one to spring into a somersault, then disappear head-first into the pool. Tad came up grinning, shaking the water from his hair. "Oh, this feels good."

He applauded. There was no way his gigantic ass was ever going to be able to do that. "Impressive!"

Tad swam over and rested wet arms on his knees. "Are you coming in? Or are you just here to watch me relive my college days?"

"Oh, I'm totally coming in. I swim damn near every day."

He slipped in, stole a kiss, and then goosed Tad. "That was damn impressive, baby."

"Ow!" Tad beamed, looking happy. "You ain't seen nothin' yet." Tad swam an effortless circle around him, like the kid was half fish. "What do you do when you swim every day? Laps?"

"Yep. Gotta keep my girlish figure." He laughed and flexed, showing off his abs.

Tad flattened a hand on his belly. "This is far, far from girlish. Laps are boring. Water is natural resistance. You should do a water workout."

"Oh, you'll have to tell me all about that. I'm always looking for a new workout."

"I will. I have much experience in this arena. But not today, today we're playing." Tad winked and swam off, headed back for the diving board. The next dive was two flips, and Tad added a rotation so he hit the water facing the other direction.

"Damn!" Okay, that was cool. He applauded again, floating idly as he watched. Part of him was jealous because he always wanted to be the person that could do anything, but he wasn't fifteen years old and crying in his room because he hadn't made varsity as a freshman.

"This is fun. Thanks for having me." Tad swam back to him, grinning. "Did your friend... Dave, was it? Did he come out here a lot?"

"Four or five times a summer, I guess? At least he had until this summer." This summer Dave had been a wreck, had been in and out of a facility.

"Was he sick?" Tad blinked at him. "Sorry. Probably not my business."

"He was, yes. He suffered from depression and cluster headaches. It sucked."

"Oh." Tad nodded, sun making him squint as their eyes met. "God, that sucks. I'm sorry."

"Yeah. Me too." Dave had been a good man—smart, funny, kind of a dipshit, but decent.

Tad leaned up and kissed him. "Okay, cowboy. Go do a cannonball off the diving board."

"At least it won't be a bellyflop, huh?" He swam across the pool and heaved himself up next to the diving board, loving the pull on his muscles.

"You can't not smile and do a cannonball!" Tad swam to the side of the pool to give him plenty of splashing room.

Strait scowled, but only for a second, because Tad was right. This was pure fucking joy. He hit the water, arms wrapped around his legs.

"Woo!" Tad was laughing and hooting when he came up. "That was awesome! You got water all the way over...look! Way over there!"

"I can displace some water, huh?" He cracked up, amusing the fuck out of himself. "Did I miss the towels?"

"You did. Very clever of you. I'd take a turn, but that was way more impressive than I could manage." Tad was all smiles. "Laps? And then maybe a nap in the sun."

"Works for me, baby." There was a great double chaise to nap in, and—A shadow caught his attention and he winced. "Duck."

He grabbed Tad and tugged about the time that his youngest dog, Bart, hit the water like a torpedo.

"Whoa! Good save. Thank you." Tad was grinning, not the least bit fazed by canine antics. "Who's this?"

"Bart. Homer is scared of the pool, and Marge is staying with Andy and Mitch since she's fixin' to pop."

"Simpsons fan, huh? I love it. Marge has pups? When is

she due? Who are Andy and Mitch? Is the sky blue?" Tad laughed and shook his head. "I'm the worst."

"Yes. Yes. Any day now. And my housekeeper/cook/valet/personal assistant/best friends. And..." He looked up. "Yes."

Tad took his face in pruney fingers, smile brighter than the sun. "Oh, you are amazing. Cooper—my best friend, you know—would have tried to drown me." He got a quick kiss and then Tad was off, to play with Bart.

Oh, Bart was going to be on Cloud Nine. A new person to play with who liked the water? Tad was going to have a drippy buddy.

He tossed over Bart's ball before he started doing his laps, moving easily through the water. Mitch was going to ride his ass hard for picking a guy up at a bar and bringing him home.

Tad and Bart played dive and fetch forever. It eventually turned into swim and chew, which then became lounge and soak up sun. By the time he'd finished his laps, the two of them were stretched out relaxing, Tad drying off on the double chaise and Bart flopped on his side on the warm concrete.

He crawled out, grabbed a couple of bottles of water and handed one to Tad. Then he stripped off his wet trunks and stretched out in the sun.

"That's how we do it here, huh? Cool." Tad set the water down and wiggled out of the tiny suit, an ancient hint of a permanent tan line cutting across the guy's trim hip as Tad stretched out on his stomach. "Just remind me to put on some sunscreen in a bit. I don't want to be out of commission. Anybody ever smacked you on your sunburned ass? Now that's fucking painful."

"Nope. I'm tan all over." And not spankable. Anyone

tried it and he'd put them over his knee and disabuse them of that urge straightaway.

"Yes, I was just admiring that fact." Tad walked two fingers up his chest. "I think I might admire some more."

"Yeah? I like how you admire, baby." He liked the way Tad focused; it made him feel ten feet tall and bulletproof.

"How did your laps feel? You looked pretty—"

"Bart! Bart, you sly beast, where the hell did you—oh." Mitch stopped dead, and the look on his friend's face would have been funny if circumstances were just a little different than they were. "Well, now. Hey, man. Sorry, I was just— Bart got away from me."

"Hey." Tad didn't give him a chance to reply, just rolled over and sat right up, offering Mitch a hand. "I'm Tad. Bart and I had a swim."

"I'm... Mitch." Mitch reached over Strait's bare ass and shook Tad's hand.

"Oh! Mitch! One of the housekeeper/cook/valet/personal assistant/best friends!"

"Right. Sounds like me." Mitch glanced at him curiously and then looked back at Tad. "You...and Bart had a swim?"

"Well, okay. Strait was swimming, we were having a catch and a wrestle."

"That sounds more like it." Mitch tugged on his ballcap. "I'll leave y'all to it. Sorry to interrupt. Bart okay out here, man?"

"He's fine. How's my girl?" He'd be damned if he got all nervy. Mitch had seen him naked before, for fuck's sake.

"Marge? As big as a house and grumpy. She is about ready to pop."

Tad flopped back onto his stomach. "I love puppies. Strait says Homer's not a fan of the pool."

"No, sir. But you can see him in the window there

watching." Mitch pointed. "He won't let anyone drown either."

"What a sweetie."

Mitch nodded. "I moved your truck, Strait. What are you thinking for dinner?"

"I was kinda thinking steaks. Y'all in, or do you have plans?" *How interested in meeting Tad are you?*

"We're in. I'll get Andy to fire up the grill in a bit. Margaritas?"

Tad leaned closer and stage-whispered, "Say yes, cowboy."

"Sounds like a plan. Seven?"

"Seven it is." Mitch nodded to him, eyes twinkling.

"Mmm. Steak. Sounds great."

"Andy is a master with meat and a grill. Prepare to be amazed. I better go scrounge up steaks. Enjoy the sunshine." Mitch headed back into the house, and Tad settled a towel over that lovely pale ass.

"I was starting to feel it a little, but I didn't want to cover up with him standing here and let him think I was embarrassed or something." When you stretched the guy out long, Tad looked taller than he seemed standing up.

"Do you need sunscreen? There's some out here." *Somewhere.*

"Not if it means getting up. This is fine." Tad blinked blue eyes at him. "Mitch seems like a good guy. Sure you're okay with me hanging out with your friends?"

"They're my right hands." He blinked. *Why on earth wouldn't he introduce Tad to the guys?* "Are you a serial killer?"

Tad laughed lazily. "Not last I checked. A serial one-night stand maybe."

"Then you're going to be good with the guys, no stress."

He figured the sooner they met Tad, the less shit they'd give him.

"Mmm. Cool." Tad's eyes slid closed, and he gave the guy five minutes to total lights out. He'd try not to brag about wearing his second-night stand out.

But that didn't mean he wasn't smug as fuck.

5

The smell of the grill woke him up. That, and Bart breathing on him from the other side of the chaise where his cowboy had been. Dog breath. Yay.

Tad found a shower in the pool house and rinsed the chlorine off, stuffed his suit in his bag, then pulled on his shorts and a why-bother tank top.

His stomach was growling at him, sternly reminding him he hadn't eaten in a couple of hours, so he shouldered his bag and headed for the house. He thought about checking his phone, but he already knew he'd find a hundred texts and a couple of missed calls from Cooper, wondering where he was, and wanting to know all about Strait.

That part he got; he wanted to know all about Strait too.

Bart followed him inside. He followed his nose and the sound of country music and men laughing. What the hell was he doing here? This was too weird. Good weird, yeah, but weird.

He turned down a hall and the voices got louder as he

found himself heading toward another wall of windows. Damn, this place was amazing.

Strait perched on a barstool, wearing a tissue-paper thin pair of jeans and a T-shirt that he could almost see through. Damn, that was hot as hell.

He tried not to let the fact that this was going to be the most embarrassing entrance ever overshadow the view. "Evening, gentlemen." He smiled and went right to Strait, trying not to look as intimidated by this group of friends he was walking into as he felt. "Evening, Sir."

"Hey, baby." Strait wrapped one arm around him and drew him in for a kiss that melted him. "I was fixin' to come get you. I put the umbrella over you so you didn't burn anything."

Don't let go yet. His skin wasn't burned but he was starting to smolder anyway. "Thank you. Bart appreciated the shade too." He leaned up, daring to take another quick kiss.

"Mmm..." Strait kept him right there, holding him close. "You've met Mitch. This is his husband, Andy."

Husband. Whoa.

He stuck one arm out, the wrong one because Strait had his shaking hand pinned against a solid rib cage. "Hello, Husband Andy. I hear you're quite the grill master. Sure smells like heaven out here."

Andy had a great smile, the dark eyes shining at him. "Someone has to feed this hooligan, right? Pleased to meet you."

"Hooligan." He smiled up at Strait. "Is that accurate?"

Okay, so no one had called him sleeping beauty or busted Strait's chops about not sleeping the night before. At least not with him around, which was cool. It was still weird though. Just...so strange to be shooting the breeze, grilling out with a date he barely knew and couple of guys he didn't know at all, just like he belonged there.

"Oh absolutely. I'm rotten." Strait rolled his eyes. "Luckily, I have charm."

"Buckets of it. I'm totally charmed." Totally. Completely. Possibly hopelessly.

Mitch snorted, filling glasses from a blender behind the bar. "Margaritas are up, Charmer."

"Oh, you do have handy friends, Strait."

Andy started handing them out and Tad reached for his, the first sip tasting more refreshing than the pool had been. "Mmm."

"Cheers, y'all." Strait lifted his glass, then took a drink, licking the salt off the rim first. That little move sent shivers up and down his spine.

"Cheers!" Andy and Mitch touched their glasses and then shared a kiss so sweet it made him wish.

"Steaks," Andy said, smiling at Mitch. On the way back to the grill, Andy touched Strait's shoulder. "I think you ought to know we're a little put out you didn't tell us you were seeing someone."

Oh, wow. Tad hid in his margarita.

"I'm sorry. I was just caught up in everything. Tad was a huge comfort last night."

Strait was pure class. Fuck him raw. Absolute pure class.

"You must have been, Tad. I didn't expect to see a smile on this guy's face again for a while. Welcome to the ranch." Mitch raised a glass to him and took a sip.

"Thank you, Mitch." He didn't really know what else to say, and he knew he was blushing like mad—*dammit*—so he tangled his fingers with Strait's and just held on.

Strait winked at him and clinked their glasses together. "How do you like your steak, baby?"

"Big?" He grinned, and Andy lost it laughing over at the grill. "Oh, gosh. And medium rare."

Mitch chuckled and ducked out from behind the little outdoor bar. "That's a keeper right there."

"No shit on that, Mitch." Strait's fingers dragged along his hip, sliding in slow, lazy circles.

He snorted. Keeper. It hadn't even been twenty-four hours yet. And maybe he didn't feel like being kept, huh? What about that?

Ha. Who was he kidding?

"How long have you guys been married?"

"Uh." Mitch squinted over at Andy. "Are we on four years, babe? Or wait...five?"

"The romance is gone. Gone, I tell you. Five years on Christmas." Andy glared at Mitch, eyebrows gyrating madly.

"It's the damn New Year that fouls me up. We got married one year and honeymooned the next." Mitch looped an arm around Andy and blew a raspberry against Andy's neck.

"Aren't they something? I've had to put up with this for years." Strait didn't sound terribly put out.

"Five, apparently. At least." Marriage. What a weird concept.

I now pronounce you Mr. and Mr. Cowboy.

Yeah...no. He didn't even understand Mr. and Mrs. Cowboy.

He understood this, though. The beautiful night, the cooling air, the arms around him. This was basically a fairy tale right here. Real life was going to suck when he had to go back to it.

"Shit, I've known Mitch my whole life. His dad is my father's right-hand man."

"Yeah?" Right. Strait said they were best friends. "That's neat. Now he's working for you, huh?"

"That's what we have on paper, anyway."

"You seem like a good employer. Maybe I should ask for a job." He gave Strait a sly look over the top of his margarita. It was a good one. Mitch mixed them strong.

"Oh now, I'm not one to mix business with pleasure."

"I'm headed in to check on the sides. Andy says the streaks are resting. You want to eat in or out, boss?" Mitch was backing slowly toward the house.

"Out, I think. It's a gorgeous night." Strait licked and sipped again.

"You got it."

"Hang on then, I'll help." Andy jogged after Mitch and the two of them went inside.

"Really, they're impossibly perfect." He set his glass down on the bar and stretched up tall, stomach growling.

"They're madly in love. It's insane, seriously." Strait chuckled, and there was something in the laugh, something he didn't understand.

He'd just add that to all the other things Strait did that he didn't understand. Honestly, he'd known the man a day? He was going to have to start paying better attention.

The guys came back and in about two minutes there was a table set, complete with candles behind hurricane glasses, a few amazing-looking sides and Andy was serving up steaks.

"Oh my god. My mouth is watering, you guys. This looks amazing."

Andy beamed at him. "Thank you. It's nice to have company."

Strait pulled a chair out for Tad. "It is."

He froze for a second, surprised, feeling warm all the

way to his toes. "Thank you, Sir." He reached for Strait's fingers where they were still settled on the back of his chair and covered them with his own before taking a seat and letting Strait push his chair in.

Strait bent and kissed Tad's temple before going to take his own seat. "You've outdone yourself, y'all. Thank you."

"You're welcome. It's not every day that you bring someone home, right?"

"It's not any day," Mitch winked at Tad. "Least not one I can remember."

Strait rolled his eyes. "Pass the rolls, butthead."

Never? Tad watched Strait make a gimme gesture with those strong fingers. Things between him and Strait were getting more interesting every hour they spent together.

"The temptation to toss one at you is strong, man." Mitch handed Strait the basket of rolls.

"Are those sweet potatoes?"

Mitch picked up the dish and handed it over. "Yep. I made them. Tell me what you think."

"Tell me what you think," Andy repeated, playfully and smacked Mitch in the shoulder. "He knows they're good, he just wants to hear you say it. His ego is almost as big as Strait's."

"Almost?" Strait snorted. "Shee-it, it's a wonder he can fit his head through the damn door."

"The sweet potatoes are delicious, Mitch," Tad said with wicked grin. "Really."

"Everyone likes them." Mitch sat back smugly and sipped his beer.

Andy rolled his eyes. "Jesus. Now you've done it. Easy for you, huh? You don't have to share quarters with him."

That made Tad laugh, and he snorted his sip of margarita, which set him giggling harder.

"You see how I'm abused, man? My man and my boss, they want to hurt me."

He nodded, cutting another bite of steak. "Quit teasing and eat." He took a bite and chewed happily. God, he was hungry. "This is so good."

"They take good care of me." Strait dug in with gusto, but that one hand kept sneaking over to touch him.

"Smart man, Tad. The food is better than the jokes." Andy took a big bite and grinned.

This just wasn't real. It couldn't be. Maybe he'd had too much to drink at the bar, and he was actually passed out in Cooper's bathroom. Wouldn't be the first time.

The next time Strait reached over he grabbed those fingers and gave them a squeeze.

Nope. This was definitely real.

Strait turned and looked at him, eyes searching his face, then he got another of those pirate smiles and a return squeeze.

Okay, then. He'd convinced himself he wasn't dreaming, now he needed to get his head around whatever that meant, what the hell happened next.

6

S trait woke up wrapped around a warm body, which
wasn't totally foreign. He just needed to know which
hotel he was in.

He opened his eyes and came right awake.

He was home, in his bedroom with a man. That
was new.

Not the man part, just the home part. Had he really
introduced this man he'd barely known for a full day to his
friends?

Shit, like that was shocking. He had decided to leave his
daddy's company to start his own on his gut feelings, had
sold his company on that same gut. He didn't doubt that he
was blessed, and he never questioned when he was called to
do something.

Tad sighed softly and tucked his arm in tighter, that mop
of blond hair falling against his chest. The kid sure seemed
happy at his place. Tad loved his pool, played with his dogs,
and fit right in at dinner.

Strait just couldn't bring himself to regret this, so he
didn't bother.

He hit the remote that opened the television cabinet, flipping through his calendar, his emails, his phone calls. It was Sunday, so there was precious little to do, barring call his mamaw and papaw.

They expected his call every Sunday at one p.m., and unless the apocalypse happened, he made it happen.

"Morning." Tad kissed his chest and yawned. "Mmm. Warm."

"Mornin', baby." He dragged one hand down Tad's back, humming deep in his chest. Such a pretty baby.

"Did you sleep? You want some coffee?" Tad rolled onto his back and stretched long. "Oh. We're at your place. Right."

"Mmhmm. I did, I do, and we are. Come on. There will be some coffee made and doughnuts on the counter." It was good to be him.

Tad sat up, blinking and looking sleepy, hair everywhere. "Can we swim before you take me back to my place?"

"Baby, we can do anything you want." He loved this, having someone he wanted to know about, to visit with.

"Awesome." Tad kissed him and climbed out of bed with a groan. "Jesus. You really are a better workout than the gym."

"You want to bubble in the hot tub while we coffee?" That would ease any sore muscles.

Those bright blue eyes caught him, lit by a flirty grin, and Tad turned toward him. "You're spoiling me now, Sir."

"That's my prerogative, baby." What good was life if you couldn't be good to somebody? Not that he was having 'gee I'm being neighborly' thoughts about Tad. No, he was bordering on the farthest of friendship before he landed in seduction. Maybe. Maybe he was just trying his dead level best to seduce Tad into a puddle of goo.

"Let me find some shorts. I'm not really a naked-in-the-kitchen type." Tad laughed and started digging through the overnight bag he'd brought.

"No?" He grabbed his pajama pants and tugged them on, in deference to the guys that popped in and out of the house.

Tad pulled on a pair of cutoffs so worn in they were basically the next best thing to naked and took his arm. "Show me to the doughnuts, Sir."

"You got it, baby." God, that view from up here made his abs tight.

"I guess it's back to the real world today, huh? What does your real world look like, Mr. Retired? What does Monday morning mean?" He thought he was supposed to be leading, but Tad was moving quickly, pulling him toward the kitchen. The kid had way too much energy for first thing in the morning.

"Tomorrow, I have a conference call with the board of directors of my company, and I've got to take my momma to lunch for her birthday. In the afternoon I'll deal with emails, and I've got to work with one of my newer horses, so I'll take Ghost out." His world was just as busy and ordered as ever, just totally in his control. "What about you?"

"Whoa. Busy busy." Tad went for the coffee pot. "Well, I try to keep Mondays open because I usually need a recovery day, but tomorrow I'll get up and work out in the morning, and then I bet Cooper will want to have brunch to find out where I was last night, and he'll want to hear all about you. After that I'll go home and get some work done. I have a website I need to build and a couple of graphics to put together for clients."

"I like people who work from home. They have

discipline. I appreciate that. Are you a runner? A gym bunny?" He only ran when he was being chased.

"I run. And I don't know about a bunny, but I like the gym. I've been thinking about training for something. A marathon, a triathlon...something. Something to work toward. Something so my dad will stop pushing me to move back to Jersey."

"Well, I have the perfect pool to train in, if you have the need." New Jersey? Seriously? It was cold there. He was a tropical man at heart. Hell, he'd been known to spend six months at a time in the islands, finding his Zen.

"Thank you, Sir." Tad handed him a cup of coffee and poured a second. "I just need to accomplish something. Something he can brag about. I think that would be enough for him."

He got that. Shit, he grew up with a daddy and a pappy that had his whole life planned—from his baby Luccheses to the underwear he had on the day he graduated. Fortunately, he had a momma that was a Boho artist type who went with him to get his first tattoo and celebrated that she had a gay son. He didn't have a response that didn't sound like bullshit though. "Everybody's got that one person they can't quite please, huh?"

"Guess so. Maybe one day. This is good coffee." Tad leaned up and kissed him. "I've just decided to look for the one person I can please."

"You are a wise man." Strait cupped Tad's jaw and held him there, sinking into the taste of his new lover, drinking deep from that well.

Tad melted into him, offering everything except the coffee mug still in one hand. That the kid tried, and failed, to set down on a counter and ended up giggling against his lips. "Damn."

He took the mug, put it aside, and leaned in. "One more before our swim, baby."

He didn't really ask, but Tad didn't look like he was complaining.

Tad blinked at him slowly, eyes gone soft. "One more, ten more, I've got time."

"So do I." Strait moaned softly, lips brushing Tad's once before he dove back in. There was something heady about a lover that kissed, something better about one that enjoyed it.

Tad sighed and opened for him so he could explore and taste, those light, graceful fingers playing over his chest. His body tightened and he forced himself to breathe, to relax and enjoy this for now. Tad wasn't in a rush to leave, so he was going to let this happen.

"I love how you kiss me," Tad whispered, so quiet he almost missed it.

"I hear that. This is something else." Something that made sense, way down in his bones.

"Impossible, and totally real anyway." Tad smiled up at him.

"Nothing is impossible, baby. I believe that." He rubbed their noses together. "Want to come swim?"

"Yes, Sir. Swim, and then we earn doughnuts." Tad grabbed one more sip of coffee and headed for the pool. The shorts got ditched en route and Tad didn't stop moving, walking right to the edge and diving into a set of laps.

Strait dropped his pants and grabbed two towels, putting them in the sun before he slipped into the water and started his own morning swim.

They had a nice workout, each of them passing and lapping the other by turns. Finally, Tad floated by him grinning. "I'm in love with your pool."

"It's a handy thing, hmm? I love coming out in the middle of the night."

"We'll have to try that next." Tad disappeared under the surface, popped up in the deep end and climbed out. "One dive, so say a prayer for the family jewels."

Tad tested out the bounce again, then launched himself backward into a twisty thing with a single somersault.

Oh look at that. That was pretty as the shine on a new bike. Tad made his mouth dry. Damn.

"Fun!" The kid swam right to him and looped an arm around his neck.

There was a round of applause from the pool's edge and they both looked over at Andy. "Nice! Sexy and talented too. Quite a catch, Strait. Y'all want some eggs? Mitch is scrambling."

"Baby? You like eggs?" Soon Andy and Mitch would know what Tad liked too.

"Morning, Andy!" Tad waved. "Yes, please."

"Good morning. That was some dive."

Tad beamed at Andy, pleased. "Just having fun, and it's been a while."

"If you say so. I'll get Mitch on the eggs. Enjoy your swim." Andy ducked back inside.

"Mitch's brunches come with mimosas and waffles usually." God, he loved Sundays.

"What? That's crazy. I am so spoiled here. That sounds great." Tad hung on him, floating lazily, cheeks flushed from a good workout.

"I don't hate it." He refused to be guilty—he'd worked his ass off, invented something that no one else had that made the world a better place and made his fortune. He was lucky, smart, and he intended to enjoy every second.

"No, I don't either. And it doesn't seem like your friends are too broken up about it." Tad laughed and pulled him toward the steps. "Quick shower in the pool house before we eat? You think you can keep your hands off me?"

"Not a chance." He would touch, even if it wasn't sexual.

Tad's smile was bright as the morning sun. "You know, I thought that was what you'd say." They climbed out of the pool, and Tad appreciated the sun-warmed towel.

"You know me already." Like anybody could resist touching that sweet ass.

"I doubt that very much." Tad winked and turned around and he followed along into the pool house. "You're complicated. I know I haven't figured you out yet."

"Just a cowboy." Sort of. Maybe just a cowboy and a little bit of an oilman. Shit, he didn't know. "Come on now, let's get washed off."

"Yes, Sir." Tad started the shower and pulled him in. "My buddy Cooper says cowboys are the worst. He says you really have to live with a cowboy to know him."

"Has he lived with many, baby?"

"Cooper? No. Just one that I know of, and it didn't work out." Ted grinned at him, flirting. "Are you saying I shouldn't put so much stock in what he has to say?"

"I'm saying that I grew up with them—they're vain, pushy, arrogant bastards, and they're some of the best people I know." He grinned right back. "Hopefully you'll think the same thing."

"Mmm. So far so good. I got some of the vain and pushy at the bar Friday night...and honestly, I wouldn't mind seeing more of that. I'm just crazy enough to make sure you know how much it turns me on."

All he remembered about the bar on Friday was Tad's

mouth, and how he'd wanted to fuck those pretty lips. "Good to know."

"I think so." Tad spent the next few minutes giving him a quick scrub and washing his hair, paying attention like it was the most important thing Tad had ever done, and nothing about all of those touches and caresses was anything more than fondness and affection.

He took it, because damn it felt good. "You're good to me, baby."

"You've been taking care of me for two days. And I enjoy this. You're very well built." Tad laughed gently, finishing up.

He flexed, letting all his muscles jump and bulge. "Thank you, baby."

He had to admit he liked having all those hours working in the barns and on the houses and in the gym noticed.

That just made his lover laugh harder and those gentle fingers more curious. "Look at that! I'll have some more, please."

He swatted Tad's ass, just a little harder than he'd intended. "Come on, you. Brunch is ready."

Tad's soft gasp made him turn his head and he caught a fleeting, glassy-eyed look that left behind a wistful smile on Tad's face. His lover scurried to grab them towels. "Yes, Sir."

Christ, that made him hard as a rock, made him need so fast he was a little light-headed.

Tad placed a towel over his shoulders. One thing he knew, the kid didn't miss a thing. Tad was making a little show of drying off, giving him a view of all that pale skin, of that tight ass.

Oh.

Oh, he could tap that ass right now. Just bend Tad over on the bench and fuck him until he begged for mercy.

"So...brunch, Sir?" Tad brushed by him, so close, and wrapped the towel around a trim waist. "Our shorts are still out there by the pool."

"Don't tease the bear, baby. I bite."

"Promise?" The pool house door opened, and Tad was suddenly steps away. "Just hold that thought for next time."

He let himself growl, let his hunger out, just a little bit. Tad shivered, which was gratifying as fuck, and he hustled Tad out to the deck.

Tad brought his sweats to him and pulled on those barely there cutoffs, staying close and waiting for him to lead them both back into the house.

He wrapped one arm around Tad, grabbed that tight ass and in they went. The kitchen smelled like heaven—maple and sausage and eggs. "Mornin', y'all."

"Mornin'. Good swim?" Mitch was just setting out food on the breakfast bar, and Andy was ready with coffee for each of them.

"I love that pool. Love it." Tad accepted a mug of coffee. "Thanks."

"Excellent. How are y'all?" The guys had off from noon today until noon Tuesday, as a rule, and he tried his damnedest to remember that.

"I'm not sure yet, Mitch has plans for our day off that he won't share."

Mitch snorted. "The lack of trust is disappointing."

"I haven't forgotten the Great Camping Disaster of twenty-seventeen." Andy laughed, serving up plates.

"Try as I might, baby, I can't control the weather."

"You can't pitch a tent either."

Tad laughed, the sound honest joy.

"Have fun. I'm going to take Ghost out tomorrow

afternoon, but I'll have my phone if y'all get stuck again..."
Strait winked at Andy and waited for Mitch to fuss.

"Oh fuck y'all." Mitch was laughing though, good and hard.

"Camping." Tad shivered, grinning. "No. Not for me. I enjoy indoor plumbing too much. And a real bed. And Wi-Fi."

"Cabins. Lots of great cabins you can rent. Very romantic." Andy stuck his tongue out at Mitch and went back to eating, but Mitch winked over Andy's head at Strait. Good man. Looked like his friend had gotten that message loud and clear.

"I require a certain amount of connection, myself." But that wasn't an issue for him, really, was it? "What's your favorite vacation, baby?"

"I like to see things. But the where doesn't matter really. The woods, the beach, a busy city, a B&B in a cute little town... I just like to go places I've never been, you know? Change it up. Experience things. Learn something."

"Our Strait just disappears for months into the Caribbean. I'm not sure he learns anything."

Strait flipped Mitch off.

Tad glanced at him, then looked at Mitch. "I bet I could teach him a few things in the Caribbean. I mean, learn something."

"You say the word, baby. We'll go. I have a home there, a private beach, a boat." He could leave tonight.

"What?"

"The house has Wi-Fi. We could leave tonight, if you want." He would always go to the island.

Mitch and Andy watched them with matching grins on their faces.

Tad stared at them for a second, then laughed. "Oh,

haha. Okay. You guys are funny. Could someone pass me a glazed doughnut?"

Strait hooked one finger under Tad's chin, brought their gazes together. He had to make one thing crystal clear. "I don't lie. Not even when it would serve me. There's a house with a private beach and a boat at the marina. We can leave tonight. I totally understand if you don't want to go, but I can make it happen."

Tad froze. "I didn't mean you were lying, I just thought you were kidding about leaving tonight and—" Those big blue eyes went wide, and Tad looked sharply down at the floor. "Yes, Sir. I'm sorry, Sir, but I can't go tonight."

The kitchen was awkwardly still for a moment and then Andy whistled. "Okay. Where are the dogs, Mitch?"

He ignored the guys, focused only on Tad. He wasn't angry, but it was important that Tad understand what was what. "Don't be sorry, baby. Everyone can't just drop everything and go. Let me know if you want to go sometime."

"Yes, Sir. I will. It sounds really nice."

Mitch, who probably knew him better than anyone, didn't seem to be the least bit uncomfortable. "One glazed doughnut and..." A small plate landed in front of him. "Half a dozen chocolate glazed doughnut holes for the big boy."

Strait grabbed one and tossed it up, snapping it right out of the air. Those had always been his favorites. Always.

Andy applauded. "Your mouth never ceases to amaze."

"Or me." At least Tad had the sense to blush.

Strait rolled his eyes. "Yeah, yeah. Buttheads. You want one, baby?"

"Yes, please." Tad snagged one and copied him, tossing it up and catching it in his mouth as well, looking smug.

"I'm out!" Mitch about lost it, giggling like a fiend before turning to do the dishes.

He applauded though, tickled as a pig in shit. He liked a man who could hold his own.

He couldn't help but notice the way Andy nodded to Tad just then. The gesture was appreciative, Andy's smile genuine, but the squint in Andy's eyes, the look that passed between his friend and Tad said something deeper. Something Tad seemed to get because his new lover nodded back.

Weird. He looked to Mitch, one eyebrow lifting, and his best friend just winked again like he knew a secret.

"Mimosas are such a treat." Tad picked one up and handed it to him. "To...hot cowboys."

"To new friends," he returned. "And old ones."

"Hear, hear!" Andy clinked glasses with them.

"Okay, that one is better." Tad leaned close and begged a kiss, and what else could he do but give it after being asked so prettily.

He moaned when Tad opened to him, and he had to force himself to ease up.

But Tad didn't pull back right away. His lover stayed close and just breathed him in for a long moment. "Wow."

"Yeah. Most definitely." Three words in a row, go him.

Tad blinked at him, smiling. "I think you better take me home, cowboy. I'm getting dangerously close to never leaving."

Oddly enough, he could learn to live with that. "Finish your eggs, baby, and I'll take you anywhere you want."

"Hey, do you want us to move Marge back up to the house while we're gone?" Mitch leaned on the counter. "We'll be back late Tuesday, but she might deliver by then. Are you sure it's an okay time for us to go?"

"I'll manage. I have Stacy on my speed dial. Do y'all have her whelping box set up or do I need to grab it?"

"It's at our place; we'll bring it up before we go."

"I still don't know where we're going." Andy sang, waving a mimosa.

"No, sir. You do not." Mitch grinned and Andy stuck out his tongue.

"I'm sensing a theme." Tad took one last bite, chewing happily. "So tasty. Thanks, Mitch."

"You're welcome, man." Mitch's smile was altogether too knowing, but it seemed pleased.

"I'm all done, Sir. Should we go get dressed?"

Andy sighed. "Aw. Do you have to? You're both pretty easy on the eyes."

Tad laughed. "Careful, your man has big plans."

"I know. I'm so lucky. These men know how to spoil a guy." Andy's words made him blush.

"I'm learning that." Tad gave him a nudge. "Come on, stud. Clothes."

"You got it. Come on, baby." He stood and waved to Mitch and Andy. "I'll see y'all Tuesday."

"I'll be here. Call if the puppies come?"

"You got it." He took Tad's hand. "Come on, you. Let's get your fine ass back to Austin."

"My ass needs pants first, Sir. Nice to meet you guys." Tad waved to Mitch and Andy, then pulled him along by the hand. "It's not really that I'm in a hurry to get back to Austin, you know. I mean I do need to get back to my laptop tomorrow but..."

"But this is a lot for a first date, hmm?" He got it. Hell, he was a lot, full stop.

Tad nodded. "It's been incredible. You've been amazing.

And I love this place and your pool and your friends...it's been wonderful. Really. Best first date ever."

"I look forward to the second." Strait stole one more kiss before heading to get dressed.

He was looking forward to more than just the second, but that was up to Tad. The next step would have to be his.

Strait sure hoped Tad called.

7

Tad was putting off calling Cooper even though he knew he needed to. Cooper had texted him a dozen times since yesterday. The poor guy probably thought he'd fallen off the face of the earth.

He sat in his living room, looking around like he'd never seen it before. He needed a sounding board, but he knew as soon as he made that call it would break the spell. He'd have to think rationally about this whole thing with Strait, and he really didn't want to. He wanted to pack a bag for the Caribbean.

He could make dinner. He could make dinner and call Cooper after. Or call tomorrow after a good night's sleep. Maybe that would be better.

He was just getting comfortable with putting it off when his phone rang, startling him so badly he just answered it without looking to see who it was.

Like he didn't know.

"Hello?"

"I was about to call the police or Rory! Did that man

kidnap you? Are you okay? Did he hurt you? I'll have Juanito put a voodoo spell on him!"

Oh, poor Cooper. He had to laugh though. "No, Coop. I'm fine. We just got lost for a couple of days. You want to come over? We can order sushi or something."

"Lost? Was it good? Are you...oh fuck it. Yes. Yes! I'll be over in a few."

"Good." He laughed, hung up the phone, and went to open some wine. Was it good? Yeah. Yeah, it was good. It was too good. Impossibly good. He didn't know which way was up right now. Cooper would be handy. Cooper would make him drop his Strait-colored glasses and touch the ground again for a while.

He was still standing in his kitchen lost in a daydream when his doorbell rang.

"Coming!" He dashed to the door and pulled it open, grinning at Coop. "Hello."

"I was so worried, man. I brought cake *and* ice cream." Coop hugged him tight. "No moans. He didn't hurt you. Good."

"No. No, he didn't, dork. Gimme." Strait was strong and hungry, but also tender, gentle. Tad took the cake and led Coop to the fridge. "He was amazing."

"For real? Tell! Everything. I'll pour."

"Deal." He set two glasses out on the counter. "His name is Strait, after King George. He lost a close friend and was coming from the funeral the other night when we met. I don't know what he was looking for, if anything, but I don't think he expected me."

"So is he a real cowboy? Is he a Dom? Did you go to his place?" Lord, Coop was ramped up something fierce.

"He's a real cowboy, and he owns a beautiful ranch in Bastrop. He's not a Dom I don't think, but he's strong and he knows what he likes. He's as toppy as they come, and he never has questioned my calling him Sir." He could teach Strait a few things though, he really thought he could.

"Wow. So he's not in the scene, just a stud. Cool." Coop propped up next to him. "Cheers."

"Cheers." He clinked glasses with Cooper and took a sip. Not bad for under fifteen bucks. "Not in the scene at all. I'm not sure he even knows what the scene is, but he's a natural."

"Wow. I—Wow." Coop grinned at him, shaking his head. "Seriously. Wow. So he runs a ranch?"

He pulled Cooper out into the living room to sit. "No! No, no. He has staff to run his ranch. He's retired. At thirty. He used to be in oil, he said. He's got a big pool and a diving board, and big dogs." And Strait was good in bed, good out of bed, every second was a dream.

"Retired? Dude! Is he like, wealthy or rich?"

"I think he's both. I think he said his dad was set too." He laughed. "Dripping with money, I think. He has a place in the Caribbean on the beach with a boat too. He wanted me to go there tonight."

The money was really nice. The house, the pool, all of it. But it wasn't the money that kept him in Strait's arms for two days. He had some of his own.

"Like tonight-tonight?" Coop looked totally gobsmacked. "Whoa. How cool is that?"

"Like I could be on a plane right now, yeah. But I said no. I had to. I'm a mess, Coop. I don't even know if I should see him again." That was a horrible thought, but it was the truth. It was impossible, had to be.

"Oh. Oh, honey. I'm sorry." Coop hugged him, one-armed. "Not as cool as advertised, huh? That so sucks."

He took another sip of his wine and then glanced up at

Coop. "Do you think there is such a thing as love at first sight? Do you think you can know you need someone almost the moment you meet them?" He had to ask; he needed to know if he was insane or hormonal or if what he felt around Strait, what he was feeling now could be real.

"I hope there is. I haven't felt it, but I hear about it, read about it." Coop took his glass and put them both down, then took his hand. "I do believe in it. I believe it's rare, but real, you know?"

He tangled his fingers with Coop's and gave them a squeeze to stop them trembling. "Is it supposed to be terrifying?"

"Is falling in love ever not, even when it's slow?"

He shrugged. "I wouldn't know." The only thing he'd ever fallen in love with was Austin.

"I fall in love a lot. I'm always a little scared."

"A lot?" He wasn't even all that good at crushes. He'd had a handful of lovers in college that were barely even friends. Rory hit his kinks but that wasn't love. Cooper was a hoot and a half in the sack, and he loved the guy as a friend—a best friend for sure—but that hadn't ever been the kind of connection he was feeling with Strait.

"Okay, maybe not a lot-a lot, but more than a couple times for sure. Does that make me stupid, you think?"

Tad rolled his eyes. "No, butthead. I was thinking maybe it made me stupid." He scooched over on the couch, not worrying at all whether he was invited, and snuggled into Coop. "So we're not stupid. That's something."

"Go us! So..." Coop snuggled right in. "You know, if your gut says it's a bad deal, you should run, right?"

"It's not saying that. It's saying a lot of other things I have to think about though. For one thing, how stupid it was to get into his truck and let him take me to Bastrop? I mean, that was stupid shit, Coop. But it turned out fine, and I met some of his friends, and I had a really good time."

"Well, at least you had your phone. Call next time, though, so we know where you are."

"I will. I'm sorry." He knew he should have, but he hadn't on purpose. He just wanted to have fun, and he didn't want to explain himself. "The other thing my gut is telling me is that I need more of a Dom, Coop. I feel like that guy is in there, but Strait doesn't know it. Thing is, even if I help him see it, I don't know if he'll...he's amazingly gentle for such a strong Top. And then I don't even know if I should try to show him. Is that right? It is fair?"

"I—I don't know. I've never been in that situation, man. Never. I wish I had a real answer. You have to be real, though, right? If he can't give you what you need, it won't last."

He knew that. The same way he knew that sitting Strait down and having a conversation wasn't going to get him what he needed either. The man wasn't going to get it that way. He felt like Strait needed to feel it, see it for himself. What he didn't know was how or if this was going to work out.

But he wanted Strait. He'd never felt so drawn to anyone, ever before. No one had taken care of him the way Strait had either, a gentleman when he wanted one, and far from it when he didn't.

He had no idea what to tell Coop. "I know what I need. I know I'm not whole without it. I don't know what to do though. Can I have my wine back?"

"Sure. We don't have to talk about it anymore, honey." Coop handed him his glass. "I was hoping for magic for you, man."

"I think it is. I think it just needs a little pixie dust." He grinned at Coop, then sipped his wine.

"I spent the night with Rory and Juanito last night. It was something else. Juanito is a drama llama, man."

"Is he? What was his deal? Was Rory into it? I was never a drama llama." Coop wasn't drama either. Coop was outgoing and up for just about anything but drama.

"I think so, a little. There was a lot of comfort going on. Weird, huh?"

Huh. "You think they're a thing now? Like a real thing?" Rory was definitely eyeing him on Friday but maybe something happened after he and Strait left.

"Don't know. Rory isn't all that open, huh? Not with me. With you maybe."

"I'll ask him. That's interesting." He ran a hand over Cooper's leg. "And what about you? Were you hoping to get something from Rory too?"

"Just a little fun. I'm not Rory's type, but he'll do in a pinch."

"Strait has a couple of good-looking friends, married guys. I could wrap you up in a bow and give you to them." He sipped his wine again, looking over the top of the glass at Coop.

"Married, huh? Whoa. That says a lot about your cowboy, right? I mean, not in the closet."

"No, he's not. Sounds like his parents know and everything." Plus Strait had more money than most, and money could make people overlook a lot. "I really wish I knew how to make this work. I want it to work, Coop."

"Are you sure it can't? If a rich guy that's decent, into me, out of the closet, and good in bed asked me out, I'd give him a shot."

"I'm not sure of anything. It's just so intense, and I'm just nervous about how I feel and about what will happen if I ask something of him he's not willing to give. What if I blow it?" He could totally fuck this up.

"How's that worse than not going for it?"

He sighed. "Because I have zero chance of hurting him by being myself if I don't."

"If he's that into you, then it's already too late, honey." Coop kissed his cheek. "You know, no matter what, I'm on your side."

Cooper wasn't discouraging Tad at all. Wasn't a friend supposed to say things like "it's way too fast" and "don't be an idiot" or something? Coop was a smart guy. He liked to joke about working in financial aid, but his job was detailed and complicated and required a brain. If Coop thought this was all wrong, he'd say so.

Yeah, he was pretty sure Coop would say so.

"I know. Thank you. I don't think not seeing him again is an option. I already miss him. I think we need a couple of days though, you know? Just a little space to make sure this isn't about something else. Like maybe comfort after losing his friend, or about me... I don't know, being starstruck or something."

Or to quiet the little devil on his shoulder who was whispering that it would take him less than an hour to pack for the Caribbean.

Of course if the offer wasn't there because he wouldn't go at first hint, then Strait wasn't the guy he thought.

"That's fair. He's got to understand that, right? Don't you think he's feeling the same way?"

"I'm not sure. He doesn't seem like a guy that questions himself much." Strait seemed totally ready to go with it.

"Well, if he believes in it then he'll wait however long you need. Either way, you're good."

"Should I text him? Just so he knows I'm thinking about him? Should I wait until tomorrow? Should I not at all? Is a phone call better? Oh my god, Coop. I have no idea what I'm doing." He wasn't much of a dating guy. He was more of a come out and play guy.

Coop pursed his lips and tilted his head. "How about a thank you, I had a great time text?"

"Yeah? Okay." He pulled his phone off the coffee table and tapped out a quick text.

Hey, there. Just wanted to say thank you. I had a great time.

He showed the text to Coop. "Good?"

"Yeah. I think so. It's...nice, but not needy."

"Okay." He hit send and sent his text off, hoping it was the right thing to do. "Are we ordering dinner? Or are we just going to eat cake?"

"Let's order sushi. It always takes forever to get here." Coop bumped shoulders with him. "I'm glad you're okay."

He dropped his head onto Coop's shoulder. "Thanks. I'm sorry I didn't check-in." Sushi would help. And maybe some TV. Normal stuff. That was what he needed, a little normal. Just enough for him to get his bearings and figure this out.

Just enough time for him to figure out how he was going to turn his cowboy into a Dom.

8

By the time the guys got home, Strait and Coyt were both fixin' to lose their minds. Marge had whelped late Sunday night.

Thirteen puppies. Thirteen.

Then Marge had a uterine rupture and ended up in emergency surgery, so Strait and all his guys were out bottle feeding every two hours.

For thirteen puppies.

He'd sent Tad a text with a picture of the puppies, but that was all he'd had time for with his sweet girl in the hospital.

Andy and Mitch came in like whirling dervishes—dervii? Dervesh?—both grabbing a whimpering puppy and a wee bottle.

"How's Marge?"

"She's good. They're wanting me to bring her home, but I want to make sure she's going to be okay." His poor big dear girl. This broke his heart, not being able to make it all better for her.

"All the pups good? They look healthy." Mitch dropped a hand to his shoulder, gave it a pat, and sat beside him.

Andy had plopped himself on the floor and had the smallest of the pups in his lap. "This gal's a little on the small side, but she's hungry. She's so sweet."

Andy was a mess with puppies. It didn't matter how many times he was told they were going to go to other homes, he always got attached to them. Bottle feeding and handling them this much wasn't going to make that issue any better.

He thought they ought to keep two of the girls and maybe one of the boys too. It depended on personalities, on how they all meshed, and they had twelve weeks to figure that out.

"So...how's the Little Merman?"

He didn't have an answer to that. He got the very polite text that didn't say a thing, so he wasn't holding his breath. He was damn pushy for a lover, and he was self-aware enough to know that. Pushy and it was important to spoil the man he was with, to show them they were special. It was old-fashioned and weird. He sort of wished he could have been born straight. "I've been busy with these guys. I sent him a picture of the pups."

Mitch nodded slowly, and he had to assume his friend picked up on the subtext. "It seemed like he liked the dogs. Did you ask if he'd be willing to come help?"

"No. Honestly, we've all been trying to keep everyone alive. Maybe I should see if he's willing." It couldn't hurt, right?

"We could use all hands on deck. Marge is going to need help too. It's going to get tougher at first when she comes home, and you know her. She's only going to want you. Maybe Andy."

"I know. And she's going to want to try and nurse these guys, even if she's all dried up. I may have her just stay with y'all."

"That's an idea. Andy is the next best thing to you. He loves her to pieces. She'll be okay. And you'd planned this as her last litter anyway, right? She outdid herself."

Mitch rolled to his feet, dropped his pup on the fed side of the barrier, and grabbed up another.

"How was your outing, Andy? Did you have a blast?" He put one baby in the pile of blankets, then grabbed another.

Andy's smile could have warmed every pup in the room. "It was lovely. We had a real bed and everything. Dressed up dinner out, dressed down breakfast in. Nobody had to pitch a tent or worry about critters. Perfect."

Mitch shrugged. "We didn't go far, just downtown."

"It was lovely." Andy traded out pups as well, sitting with the next one and cuddling it to his chest.

"I'm tickled shitless. Y'all deserved that. Good job, buddy. Seriously." He loved when Mitch went out of his way to spoil Andy. "Ten puppies down, three to go."

"We brought food for everybody. It's in the kitchen." Mitch looked him over. "Have you slept? Showered? Why don't you go eat? We've got this."

"You sure?"

"Boss."

He chuckled, because he and Mitch had that in common. They both liked being sure. "Okay. I'll take my phone. Y'all be good."

He picked himself up off the floor, brushed the hay off, and headed into the house. There was food waiting, but he grabbed a coffee and headed to the bedroom to clean up and call Tad.

Just in case the man might want to come help.

Tad answered after a couple of rings but sounded like he'd been running. "Hey! Hey there."

"Hey. You busy?" He wasn't calling to bother the man, after all.

"Just finishing my workout. How are you? Those puppies are so cute."

"It's been a hellish few days, but we're hanging in there." He ought to go get in the pool, just float and pretend that was a workout.

"Wait. Hellish? What's going on?" He heard the music disappear, so Tad must be in the locker room now or outside.

"Marge had a uterine hemorrhage and had to have surgery, so we've been feeding newborns every two hours." Thank God and Greyhound he had help.

Tad gasped, and it felt good to know the kid was concerned. "Oh, Strait. I'm so sorry. Is she okay?"

"She will be. She's still in the hospital. I—" *Wanted to see you.* "—wanted to check in with you."

"Hey, are you okay? Do you need—if you want I—I don't have plans."

Strait found himself nodding, even though Tad couldn't see him. "Yes, please. I would welcome your help."

"I can drive out. I just need to go home and shower. Text me your address so I don't get lost?"

"Absolutely. The gate code is 9033." He forced himself to calm down, breathe. He needed to chill the fuck out. "I'll see you later, baby. Thank you."

"Be there soon. I can't wait to see you. Really." The line went dead.

Oh. That probably shouldn't feel so fucking good, but it did.

He texted his address to Tad, and then texted Mitch.

He's coming

Good man. Shave.

He knew Mitch was rolling his eyes. *On it. Asshole :)*

That's the spirit. Pups are fed. You want me and Andy to go pick Marge up? Or wait for tomorrow?

He dialed Mitch's number and put him on speaker so he could shave. As soon as Mitch answered, he responded to the question.

"Are you asking because Andy's crawling up your ass? She's just chilling out there. Stacy called about an hour ago and said she could come home tonight or tomorrow morning. I wanted to give y'all a chance to get home."

"Andy's...right here. And yes. You know." Mitch trying to talk around Andy was pretty damn funny. "But if you want to be with Tad then..."

"I want her with people she loves. Y'all go get her and bring her home. You know she loves Andy more than anything." He wasn't stupid. Andy adored Marge, and that would heal her faster than anything.

Mitch sighed, sounding relieved. "Thanks, Boss. That's very helpful."

"She's been through hell, buddy. I thought I was fixin' to lose her." Thank God he'd been there with her. He'd just been shocked that there had been so many puppies that he'd sat there stunned.

"Not on our watch, Strait. You got her to the right place. Listen, man. We've got this tonight. Eat and get some rest. Enjoy your man. We'll see you in the morning. The work will still be there."

"I will. Y'all rock." He hung up and tugged off his boots. He'd shower and shave, then nap on the sofa until Tad showed or it was time to feed, whichever came first.

Lord have mercy. What did it say about him that he was exhausted and revved because Tad was coming out?

As it turned out he got in a nap and a feeding before the knock came at his door. He opened it, and Tad was standing there all smiles, in jeans, a white T-shirt and sunglasses, blond hair tamed neatly. "Hello, Sir."

"Hey, baby." He pulled Tad in and took himself a gentle kiss.

Tad leaned close and returned the kiss, hands coming to rest on his hips. His lover didn't ask for more, but a hint of heat simmered underneath like a promise.

Damn, it was good to see him. Better to feel him. "You're a sight for sore eyes."

"You have sore eyes, all right. You look like you haven't been sleeping. Are you okay?" Tad bent to pick up a laptop case and hitched a duffel higher on his shoulder. He felt like it was more than the kid needed for an overnight stay.

"It's been a hard few days. Come stow your gear in the bedroom, and I'll take you down to meet the puppies." He eased the duffel off Tad's shoulder. "You been okay, baby?"

Tad put a hand on his chest. "I missed you." The rest of the words came out in a rush. "I'm sorry, I know that's probably a lot of pressure, and it's too soon to say stuff like that, but that's where I'm at, and I don't want to lie to you about it."

"I'm glad you're here." He'd thought about Tad every fucking day. "Real glad."

He got a bright smile, and he watched Tad relax. He could actually see Tad's shoulders ease and the change in posture. He could already read his lover like a book. "So. Put my stuff down and then puppies!"

"You know it. Mitch and Andy went to pick up Marge. Bart and Homer have been sleeping in here. I think they're worried they're in trouble." He led them back into the master and put the bag down. "You can put the computer wherever. The Wi-Fi password is my cell number."

"I just—in case I'm here and I need to work I thought it would be a good idea. Thanks." Tad tucked the bag in next to his dresser and took his hand. "Maybe they're worried about you. Bart and Homer?"

"I'm sure, and the smells have to be horrifying." He pulled Tad in for one more kiss. "I thought Andy was going to barf until I showered."

"He's funny." Tad snuggled right into him.

"He's a hoot. And Mitch adores him." He didn't want to talk about Andy, though. He wanted to introduce Tad to his puppies.

"Okay, buster, you're cute, but I bet those pups are cuter." Tad scooted around him and gave him a tug.

"You'll be surprised how little a dog that huge can start." He led Tad out to the little barn, the pups sleeping in a pile.

One of the drovers, Coyt, was obviously on puppy duty, playing on his phone while they were quiet. When they came in, he put it away and stood. "Boss."

"Hey, there. Coming to check on them."

"Hi. I'm Tad." Tad gave a wave but caught sight of the pups and gasped. "Oh, Strait! They're so little."

"Coyt. Pleased. They're gonna start looking for supper in a minute, Boss. You watch. Mitch and Andy back with their momma yet?"

"Not yet. They're taking it easy. Everybody doing okay?"

Tad had just waded in, was oohing and aahing over the puppies.

"All healthy. All hungry, Boss."

"Strait, they're so cute I can't stand it." Tad scooped one up and loved on it. "Oh my God."

"That's number four." They'd marked each one with permanent marker to keep them straight until they weren't just lumps of fur.

"Does she usually have so many pups at once? It seems like a lot. Poor thing." Tad traded out number four for number seven, but four put up enough of a protest that Tad ended up with one in each arm.

Coyt checked the time on a big wristwatch. "I'll prep bottles."

"She's had six, four, and three. This came out of nowhere." He sighed and scooped up two babies. "Not even the vet suspected."

"This is crazy. She'd probably have had trouble nursing them all regardless. Will they grow fast?"

"Like weeds. You'll be able to watch them grow over the next few months." Months. Listen to him.

"I can't wait." Tad didn't even blink.

Coyt came in with bottles, an armful of them. "Y'all ready for the madness?"

"Bring it on." Strait could feed two at a time if he used his chin to hold one of the bottles.

"Oh. Wow. Okay." Tad plopped down on the floor, stuck the two pups he was holding into his lap and reached for a bottle. "So cute. But I can see how this would get old after doing it every couple of hours."

"Thank you for your help. I appreciate it." He pushed the words through his emotions.

If Tad noticed, his lover didn't let on. He just got a nod and a smile. "Of course, Sir. I'm glad I can help. Plus, it seems like you need every set of hands you can get."

"My other option is calling in my folks, and no one wants that." Momma and Pop were good and upstanding folks, but...no.

Tad laughed. "No. Parents are great for...um. Well, I'm sure they're great for something, but stressful situations? No."

"They're good at Christmas dinner." Coyt's laugh always sounded like some weird bird.

"There. See? I knew there had to be something." Tad just kept giggling and traded out bottles and puppies. "I'm sure they're great people, Strait. I'm just teasing."

"They are, but...this is my place." And he didn't need interference. He worked damn hard at anonymity.

"I hear that. I wouldn't want my parents in my apartment. God, I'd have to... I don't know, call in a stager or something. Forbid Coop to stop by."

Strait chuckled softly, but he could see where that was a problem. Tad had a sweet little bachelor pad. "That your buddy from the bar?"

The fuckbuddy?

"One of them. The guy you met at the bar was Rory, he's...less of a buddy and more...uh." Tad blushed, which was sweet. "Well, I told you about him and me, right? Cooper was the guy I was dancing with. He's my best friend."

"He seemed like it." Good. He wanted to keep Tad busy enough not to need more 'uh'.

"You'll meet him soon enough. Hopefully you'll like him because if you're stuck with me, you're stuck with him. Unless we're in the Caribbean I guess." Tad winked at him. "Or maybe even if we are."

"There are guest rooms, no worries." He put two fed puppies back and grabbed two more. "The vet will be in to check and weigh tomorrow."

"They all seem pretty good to me. Hungry, active... considering they're stumbling around. Do you have people who want to see them, or do you wait on that until they're closer to an age where they can go?"

"I'll wait. Andy is in charge of that. I want to keep a few for us. After all, we need to have new puppies…"

"I guess Marge is done, huh? She did pretty damn well for her final litter." Tad fed the pup in his lap diligently.

"She was done anyway, but now? For sure. My poor old girl." She was six now, and time to retire and live out her life in luxury.

"It sucks right now, but I don't feel too bad for her long term. She'll recover and then everyone will treat her like the queen she is. She'll own this place if she doesn't already." Tad set the squirmy puppy down and moved on to the next.

"She totally does, mister." Coyt snorted. "That gorgeous beast is a lover and a half."

"You got that shit right, buddy." He grinned at Tad, bumped shoulders with him. "I got Homer and Marge both at the same time. Homer is a scaredy-cat, a real gentle giant. Bart's our goofball."

"I had a good time with Bart. I can see us being buddies. Homer is the one that doesn't like the pool, right? He's so sweet though. He sat right up against my leg after dinner."

"He's a lover." A dear, good obedient boy.

Coyt groaned as he bent to pick up a pup and they could hear his hips creak. "I got the last one. Damn, that was light work with three people."

"You've got one more shift, right? And then I'll be back out." That would at least give him a four-hour break.

"Jo and Helena are taking eight, ten, and twelve."

"I'll be here at two, then." He nodded to Coyt. "Thank you, man."

"Not tonight, Boss. Mitch said he and Andy had the

overnight, and you'd be in with Tad here for the eight a.m. He asked me to make sure."

"Those boys spoil me. Thank you." He would text Mitch and make sure Marge was stable enough for that.

"They know you need sleep. I can see it too. You look stressed. Have you eaten? Let's go get you some food." Tad stood up and carefully got clear of the puppies. "You have to take care of yourself before others or you're no good to anybody. Right?"

"That's the rumor." He stood and took Tad's hand, nodding to Coyt before heading out. "The guys brought food. I'm not sure what, but they said food."

Tad gave Coyt a wave as they headed back toward the kitchen and tucked into his side. His lover felt good there; they fit together perfectly. "Good. Then feeding you will be easy."

"Thank you for coming out, baby." He kissed Tad's temple, the skin there so soft. God, he did love how Tad smelled. He'd dated men that smelled bad to him, but it never worked out.

"I'm glad you texted. I wanted to see you, so this worked out great. I can see you, be helpful with the puppies, and I can take care of you too." None of that sounded like any great imposition to Tad at all.

He didn't know what to say, honestly. Wasn't it his job to spoil Tad?

Tad sat him down in the kitchen. "Looks like there's coffee. And it looks like a barbeque feast! Ooh. Brisket and beans and...okay, come on over and make yourself a plate, there's too much for me to guess."

"They would have put the potato salad and the coleslaw in the fridge. The tea's in there too." He grabbed two glasses and two plates.

Tad came back from the fridge balancing the tubs in one hand and the tea in the other like a pro. "This looks so good. I think I can hear your stomach growling."

"It smells amazing. I didn't even think I was hungry." He traded a plate for the tea. "You like barbecue sauce?"

"Yep. I'm still a Yankee that way." Tad took the plate and started filling it up, not shy about being the first to dig into the potato salad. "But I'm good without, too."

"We have spicy and not." He didn't judge. Andy loved to dip the hot stuff. "I like the sauce on a baked potato."

"Spicy, please. But potatoes are for butter and sour cream. Maybe bacon." Tad pushed the salads over to him, encouraging him to take some. "So...good thing we didn't run off to your beach house, huh?"

Strait chuckled. Yeah, yeah, yeah. He would have just turned around and come home. Marge was his girl. "You must have had a psychic moment. Although I swear to God, as soon as we can, we ought to go. It's a magical place."

Tad surprised him, agreeing readily. "I'm ready when you are."

"Excellent. I'll give the puppies until their eyes open, and they're walking, then we'll go. Can you stay a few weeks?"

"As long as there is Wi-Fi I can stay, sure. I'll have to work some. But mostly, I think it'll be a good place to...learn more about each other."

"I can't function without Wi-Fi." He handed Tad the sauce. "It's spotty on the boat, but solid in the house. I'll show you pictures later."

After food and rest and kisses. Possibly an orgasm.

"I'd like that." Tad poured out some sauce and grabbed some bread, then took a seat at the table. "I'm going to gain a thousand pounds hanging out with you."

"You have the pool and the gym at your disposal. You'll be fine." Fat? He doubted it. He got brisket and coleslaw, with a generous helping of onions and pickles.

"You're right. Bring on the no-guilt seconds." Tad grinned at him and took a big bite, talking with his mouth full. "Mmm. So good. Mm-m!"

He nodded and dug in, focusing on the food, on feeding his snarling belly. Lord, his stomach had been gnawing on his backbone.

"So, was Coyt really saying the guys gave you the night off?" Tad was eating well, like his lover had all last weekend.

"Yeah. They're good men. Honestly, sometimes I think they're just letting me play cowboy because I'm the boss."

"Does it matter? You *are* the boss." Tad winked at him, and the grin that went with it had a wicked little twist in it.

"No shit on that." That fact he was crystal clear on.

Tad twisted a couple of fingers into the front of his shirt, flirting. Or maybe seducing. Or both. "I haven't forgotten, Sir."

"Good boy," he murmured, leaning down to take another one of those kisses that he craved, storming Tad's mouth like he was a motherfucking Marine.

Tad made a soft sound, something like a sob or a whimper, and...yielded to him. He felt like he could have anything he wanted from Tad in that moment. Anything at all.

He stood and grabbed Tad's ass, driving them back a few steps until they were pressed against a wall, so he could touch, take.

Tad gasped and arched, fingers clutching at his biceps, like his lover was hanging on for dear life.

That sure as hell wasn't a no, so he just kept on keeping

on, tongue-fucking Tad like there wasn't anything else he'd rather do.

Tad moaned against his mouth, those narrow hips rolling into him and muscular shoulders pressed into the wall for leverage. He held Tad's ass, driving them together. Fuck, he was hungry. He'd been dreaming about this for days.

He felt Tad's fingers tug on his belt, but there was barely any daylight between them, and his lover gave up, untucked his shirt instead, and slid trembling fingers up under it to rest against his abs.

"Come to bed." It wasn't a request. It was a hunger.

Tad exhaled hard. "Yes, Sir."

He damn near dragged Tad to his bedroom, needing to bury himself in his baby, feed their need.

Tad finished what he'd started, working the buttons open on his shirt, sliding warm fingers over his abs and kissing his chest. "You smell so good."

"Good. Damn, baby. I want you." Bad, as a matter of fact.

"You can have me. You can have anything you want." Tad started to undress.

"I want everything." Anything? Damn. "I want your mouth, baby. I been dreaming about it."

"Yes, Sir." Tad reached for him and pushed his shirt off his shoulders, then gently loosened his belt and opened his fly. "Can't wait to taste you."

He watched Tad, the sight of those smart fingers on his cock registering before he actually felt the touch. The dissonance made him shiver.

Tad knelt down carefully and pushed fabric out of the way, baring his balls and leaning into bathe them with a curious tongue.

"Damn, baby." He spread as far as his jeans would let

him, forcing himself not to rock into the hot little touches. Lord have mercy, that was hotter than a two-dollar pistol.

"Whatever you want, Sir. I'm yours."

His?

Tad circled the head of his prick and drove a hot tongue through the slit, then opened and let him slide between those sweet lips.

"Pretty baby. You got a mouth made for this." He rubbed the corner of Tad's lips with his thumb, pushing forward in one slow move.

Tad hummed, looking up at him with bright blue eyes, fingers curling around his thighs.

"I could tear your ass up." Lord have mercy, those eyes. Those pretty eyes. He pushed deeper, backed up, then dipped in again, his sight going fuzzy.

Tad looked away, changing the angle and swallowed him down, encouraging him, asking for more.

"Fuck." He grabbed the back of Tad's head, tangling his fingers in Tad's hair. A growl tore out of his chest. "You good, baby?"

Please say you're good. I need this.

He was pretty sure he got as much of a nod as Tad could manage, and the kid's fingers dug into his thighs and held on.

That worked for him. He drove in, fucking that hot, wet mouth like a desperate man. His thighs went tight, the quads hard as rocks as he humped into his baby.

Tad held on, eyes closed, grunting and sucking in breath. That willing mouth letting him take what he needed, over and over again.

He bit a sound which might have been a warning as his balls drew up, that familiar pressure ratcheting up.

Tad hummed around him adding sensation, the sound low, the vibration against the head of his prick maddening.

Strait let himself go, trusted Tad enough to give himself over, to know that Tad could take him. His orgasm flooded his senses, leaving him wrung out, empty.

Tad released him but continued to nuzzle and lick and soothe him with warm fingers, gentle attention while his lover got a breath.

"Damn, baby." He was shaking, suddenly fucking exhausted. "I needed that bad."

"Lie down, Sir." Tad rose slowly and steered him to his bed. "Close your eyes."

He began to protest, but Tad's hands were busy, pulling his boots and jeans away, stroking his skin as it was bared. Oh lord, that was nice. "Gotta take care of you, baby."

"You will. I'm not going anywhere." Tad pushed him into the pillows. "I'm taking care of you right now."

"Mmm…" He blinked up, but his sight was fuzzy, his body insisting that he was warm, comfortable, and sated.

"Nothing like all that worry and thirteen babies to wear you out." Tad settled with him, resting in the curve of his shoulder. "And one naughty boy."

"Missed you, baby. So glad you came." He kissed Tad's forehead, his temple. "And I can handle naughty. I got me a firm hand."

"I know." Tad sighed sounding a zillion miles away. "That's why I came."

9

Tad loved how his voice sounded so blown out after having Strait's cock down his throat. He loved that he could make Strait lose it, let go, trust. He loved how Strait called him "baby".

He loved that he was lying here with Strait spent and sleeping and he'd woken up still wanting. It helped keep him floating, kept him focused, let him think about how he was putting his own needs second and Strait's first.

It was service, whether Strait understood that or not.

He hadn't meant to fall asleep at all, but Strait's rhythmic breathing and magnetic warmth had put him right out for a while. It was dark now, Strait's room full of shadows that he was still getting to know.

"Mmm..." Strait stretched long and slow, a soft, silken moan escaping the tan throat. Without a second's hesitation, Strait reached for him and drew him closer.

"Mhm." He loved that too. Being looked after, being wanted. He tucked an arm over Strait's chest—well, as far as he could reach anyway. Strait had a lot of chest. Strait was built like a brick shithouse—broad shoulders trailing down into a little ass, a ripped belly, a thick, heavy cock.

He already had the hottest lover on the planet. Now he just needed to make him into the hottest Dom. He had a plan, and he didn't think it would be that hard to do, really. But he was going to have to put aside convention and work with the man he had.

That was cool. He was all about being creative.

One of Strait's hands slid down over his back to cup his ass, the motion utterly possessive.

He leaned into the touch, liking it, but also rewarding like he was BF Skinner, and Strait had pushed the right lever.

"Baby..." Strait squeezed him, dark eyes opening halfway. "Mmm, you okay?"

"So good, Sir." Wow. He sounded a little like he'd swallowed sandpaper. "Are you?"

"Fine as frog hair." Strait's eyes opened, focused on him. "Did I hurt you, before?"

Wow. How to answer that question?

"My throat is kind of sore." He smiled at Strait, hoping the high he was still on showed in his eyes. "You were amazing."

Strait leaned up on one elbow and searched his eyes, looking hard. Tad didn't let the smile fade, and Strait must have found what he needed, because Strait took his lips with a kiss intended to steal his breath.

His surprised cry was muffled in the kiss, and he caught the back of Strait's neck with one trembling hand. The cowboy's kiss made him dizzy in an instant and he relaxed, inviting Strait in.

Strait hummed, the sound deep, low, part growl, part

song. One of those square hands stroked his skin, exploring him steadily, firmly.

God. He arched into the touch, gasping against Strait's lips. He could pretend like he was giving up control, but the fact was he didn't have it to give. Strait took it with that kiss. "Strait." The rasp in his voice made him sound even more needy.

"Yeah, baby. I got you." Strait watched him like a hawk. "So pretty."

Hot fingers wrapped around his balls, surrounding them.

"Oh." Big hands. Was there anything about Strait that wasn't perfect? He moaned as his cock stretched and strained and he slid his fingers over Strait's chest, finding a nipple and rolling it in his fingers.

"Mmm..." One of Strait's fingers began stroking behind his balls—strong, steady touches that lit up him inside.

He made a crazy, desperate sound, and he knew he probably was too easy, but Strait made him so hot, so fast and he just couldn't help himself. He didn't even want to. He'd give Strait anything. "Fuck. So good."

The touch continued with the same pressure, the same rhythm, and goose bumps popped up all over his skin.

"Please." He rocked against Strait finding some sweet contact against that incredible six-pack and begged another kiss.

"Ask so pretty." Strait stormed his mouth. Jesus, those kisses distracted him from his cock, almost.

He wasn't even sure how to return a kiss like that. He felt like all he could do was try to keep his head above water. He just held on, trusting that Strait wouldn't let him drown, humping shamelessly against the man like a horny teenager.

Tad wasn't sure when Strait got the lube, slicked himself up, but he sure noticed when two thick fingers pressed in deep, spreading him wide.

"Oh god." Strait knew just how to make him need. He arched into Strait's hand, trying to ride the cowboy's fingers, his body begging for more.

"There you go, baby." Strait leaned up, finger-fucking him, watching him with eagle eyes. "Take what you need."

"Yes... Sir." He didn't need to think about that. He rocked back with a groan and dropped one hand to his aching prick, gasping at the hot touch as he closed his fist and started to pump.

"Mmm..." Strait pressed in harder, driving into his body in time.

His eyes flew open wide. "Fuck!" A couple more jabs to just the right spot and he was flying, shuddering, soaking his fingers and gulping air.

"So fucking pretty."

He was still flying when Strait cleaned him up, hands surprisingly gentle on his skin.

"Thank you, Sir." Fuck, he'd never felt so...well, naked. He'd just let Strait have every secret little bit of him, and it felt great, but he also felt a little tender, like new skin exposed to the sun. He wanted to crawl inside Strait and be safe. He wanted Strait's arms around him.

He pressed his face to Strait's neck and breathed his lover in.

Strait sighed for him, the sound soft and sweet, and then the long arms wrapped around him and held him tight.

"You feel so good." Strait's arms were heavy and warm, more comforting than any blanket, and Tad felt like he belonged right here.

"I do. I feel like a million bucks." Strait winked at him, playing with him gently.

Tad laughed. "You had a million bucks before I came along."

Strait chuckled. "Details, details. I suppose I could feel like a gazillion bucks."

"Did you get some rest? You looked like you were sleeping pretty hard." He slowly drew his fingers across Strait's chest exploring the feel of hard muscle and soft hair.

"I crashed like a crashing, burning thing. I needed it, though. Are you hungry? Thirsty?"

"I could pick at the barbeque again, but I'm so comfortable right here. You had me out of my mind, Sir." Totally shameless. It was almost embarrassing, except that Strait obviously enjoyed watching.

"I wanted you something fierce."

"And then you took care of me, just like you said you would." Tad kissed Strait's neck. "Sent me right to the moon."

"That's my pleasure." Strait lifted his chin, offering him more.

Listen to that. "Your pleasure. Yes, Sir." Strait was already so toppy; Tad just needed to teach Strait that the things the man deeply wanted, things that Strait probably wasn't used to indulging, were actually things Tad earnestly needed. Such a small but important detail.

Strait hummed as he held Tad, rocked them to some melody playing inside Strait's head.

"Tell me more about your beach place. You said you have a boat? Is the house right on the beach?" As soon as Strait was ready to leave those puppies, he was ready to go.

"It is. The boat's docked close by. If we want it I just call, and the guys bring it. The house is simple. The main floor has the great room and the kitchen. It opens out to the beach. The second floor is my room. It's open to the weather when I want—the walls retract, and there's mosquito netting that I can open if I need it. It's just a place to completely relax—no neighbors, no family, just sun and sand."

He had people to bring his boat to him and he had no neighbors... Strait really was a millionaire. Probably a billionaire. Strait's fortune made his dad's money look like pocket change.

"Sounds like absolute heaven. What do you do with yourself down there all alone?" Like he had to ask. Strait was so hot the man probably had enough people on speed dial to never be lonely.

"The last time I slept and worked on a new concept. I need a place to get out of my head and the beach house is just a blank slate."

A blank slate.

Could there be a more perfect place to train his Dom? It was like fate. Like it was meant to be. Like...what was that word Coop used all the time?

Kismet.

"Count me in. Do you ever bring the dogs? I guess you can't really. You must miss them."

"I do, but the family who does the upkeep of the house brings their dogs over to spend time when I need it." Strait kept petting him, and the strokes were maddening, sensitizing his skin.

"You keep giving me goose bumps, Sir. Which you must know since every time I get them you smooth them down again."

"Mmm...you are damn responsive, baby. Inspiring,

even." Strait kissed his temple, scraping him with that heavy stubble.

He reached up and scritched gently at Strait's cheek, fingernails making a rasping sound. "You grow this fast, huh? It's amazing."

"I got my fair share of testosterone, that's for sure." Strait chuckled. "I swear to God, I was the fourteen-year-old with a five o'clock shadow."

"Were you really? I was madly in lust with a boy in tenth grade who could grow a beard. Me? I wanted one at fifteen, and I'm still trying to grow it." Tad laughed. He could go days without shaving. Three at least.

Strait took his chin, those dark black eyes staring at him. "I like you clean, baby. It suits you."

"Good thing, because I don't really have much say about it." He laughed, holding Strait's eyes, wondering about the brilliant mind behind them.

Strait managed to be confident without being the slightest bit cocky. Strong without being rough. It was charming as hell, and more than a bit of a turn on.

"You want to go finish our dinner, cowboy? Maybe add a margarita or something? Put our feet in the pool?"

"Sounds amazing. I have been known to make a margarita or two in my day." Strait grinned, eyes crinkling up.

"Awesome, I've been known to drink three or four." He kissed Strait's cheek and slithered off the cowboy's lap. "Ooh. I still feel those fingers."

"Good." Strait watched him walk away. "You walk like you've been well-fucked. It's a good look for you."

"Thank you. I'm counting on you to keep me that way." He gave Strait a coy smile and dug through his bag for a bathing suit.

Strait's laughter was full and rich, making him feel sexy as hell, and completely desirable.

He pulled his suit on and tugged a T-shirt on with it, breathing in that feeling, letting it settle into his skin. Then he reached for Strait and gave his lover a tug. "Come on, Sir. Tequila is calling."

"I'm right behind you, baby. I'll lube you up."

It was his turn to laugh. He was already pretty well lubed.

10

———

Strait sucked in a deep breath, the saltwater burning his nose and bringing him right home. God help him, he loved it out here.

He'd never be able to give up the ranch, the responsibilities, his family, but this was his shelter, his retreat, and he needed it like he needed air.

Tad had gone to explore, and he'd taken off his boots and headed out to stand on the back porch and breathe in the ocean.

There were beaches in other places, many of them much easier to get to. There were hundreds of miles of coastline along the Gulf, countless more in Mexico, but there was something about this place, the bright color of the water and the soft, white sand that called to him.

He was fixin' to switch out his jeans for loose pants and his felt for a straw. That was when he'd be here, all the way.

Tad came into view, trudging up the beach along the waterline. His lover was bare-chested, shoes in one hand and jeans rolled up to mid-calf. He watched as Tad let the tide roll up and drift away again, burying those bare feet in wet sand.

They'd spent most of the last two weeks in each other's pockets, and he'd never enjoyed anything more.

Well, except for now.

His lover and the beach house together? Damn.

Tad turned around and spotted him, giving him a wave and a huge grin before running to him, feet kicking up sand. "This is amazing!" Tad took a second to get the sand off his feet, then bolted up the porch steps and into his arms. "I can't believe this."

"Hey, baby." He took a happy kiss, loving the light in Tad's eyes. "You like what you see?"

"Like it? It's incredible. It's so beautiful. Look at this view!" Tad leaned against him, looking out at the water. "This is real, right? Wow."

"This is real. You should see the sunset. It's magical." He liked to watch it from the endless pool outside the bedroom.

They relaxed there a while just taking in the peace of the place, but Strait knew it was only a matter of time before Tad got twitchy.

"Show me the rest of the house! I want to see everything."

"Come on, baby. It's pretty simple and great, all at once." The bottom floor was a huge open space with a number of places to relax, read, watch movies, and it flowed into the kitchen. "The four doors are pantry, laundry room, bathroom, and office. I keep the computers in there to remind me to unplug."

"Oh cool. That's where I'll put mine too, then. I'm going to have to work eventually, but this week I told everyone I'm on vacation." Tad poked his nose in every room. "Nice. You could sleep in the pantry."

"Yes. Whatever you need from the market, leave a note. Julia and Warren will go get it." He grabbed their bags and headed toward the stairs.

"Jesus, Strait. You have people everywhere." Tad trailed along behind him. "Do they cook for you and everything? Like the guys?"

"They bring over food, but I grill a lot too. They stock me with fruit, sliced meat, bread, cheeses. Lots of cold shrimp, conch salad. Beach food."

God, his bedroom was his glory—a huge bed, a glorious bathroom, and moving walls that led out to the little endless pool.

He waited until Tad cleared the top step before he hit the buttons that opened the glass walls and the bug netting, exposing the open-air view.

"Oh my God." Tad moved into the room stepping right up to where the walls had been and just stared, looked out at the pool, up and around where the walls had been. "Strait."

"I love it here. It's like I said, a blank slate to dream on." Strait followed and wrapped his arms around Tad's waist, looking out over his shoulder at the ocean.

"To be who we want to be. It's the most beautiful place I've ever been. The most romantic. The most interesting. The best company." Tad leaned into him and sighed.

"I'm glad you're here." He had brought David here, last year, but Tad was his lover, and this was a blessing.

"I feel spoiled. I don't know whether to jump in the pool or raid the pantry first." Tad laughed. "Maybe I should kiss you."

"You should totally kiss me. It's been minutes." He loved this, making Tad smile for him.

"Oh, how could I make you wait so long?" Tad reached

back with one hand and pulled him down, the kiss as real as it was playful. "So much better. Maybe we should unpack and stay awhile."

"We totally should. Everything is behind sliding doors." He slid one back exposing a dresser, another for a closet. "There's a TV too. Somewhere."

"Oh my God, it's like the Price is Right!" Tad ran over to a sliding door. "What's behind door number three, Monty?"

The door exposed a wet bar, all set up with rum, juices. This was like watching Tad open Christmas presents.

"What? A bar in the bedroom? Shut. Up." Tad left that door open and went after another, finding the television. "Ah-ha! I have a pool, a TV, and a bar. I will never need to leave this room. As long as you are in it with me."

"Only if there's a microwave to make popcorn." He stripped off his jeans, finding a pair of loose, soft, worn cotton pants.

"You don't even know?" Tad closed the TV cabinet and went back to the bar. "Right here, Sir. Above the sink. We're golden. Oh, you're getting comfy. Cool. I'm going to find some shorts."

"I have to admit, baby. I probably won't put on boots and jeans until we're ready to leave." He was going to spend hours wet, in the sun, and making love.

"Yeah? You could leave the shirt off, that would be okay too." Tad stripped and pulled out those barely there cutoffs he'd seen before.

"Fair enough. I won't burn." He patted that sweet ass on his way by.

Strait heard Tad sigh. "That was nice, but I bet you could do better."

Better? He went back over what he said as he

unbuttoned shirt, but he couldn't figure out what Tad meant. "Sorry, honey, but I don't follow."

"That little pat. It was nice. But kind of too nice, you know?" Tad dropped the shorts to the floor and stalked him, slowly moving closer. "Didn't you tell me you had a firm hand?"

"I did." He had known a couple guys that wanted a little slap and tickle during sex, but not outside the bedroom. Not that they were outside the bedroom. Huh.

He stepped right into Tad's motion, meeting him and stopping him where they were. His hand landed on Tad's ass, maybe a little harder than he'd intended.

Tad leaned into him, humming softly, fingers playing across his chest. "That's...better. I like that. But I still think you've got more." Tad nipped at his chin. "Don't you?"

"You know what you're asking for, baby?" Did he?

Tad reached back and covered his hand pressing it harder against that round little ass cheek. "I need a spanking, Sir. Not a playful one." Tad's voice dropped to a whisper. "A dirty one. A hard one."

"Jesus." He groaned, trying to make about a thousand decisions at once. Good thing that he knew how to do that. Still... "Be sure, baby. You're damn special to me."

"I'm sure." Tad's fingers were trembling now where they covered his, and the look in his lover's eyes was pleading. "I need you. Please, Sir."

"I got your back, baby. Over the edge of the bed." He didn't waste time flipflopping. That wasn't how a man got shit done.

"Thank you, Sir." Tad didn't hesitate either, going right to the bed and folding over it with a sigh, that pale little ass offered right up to him.

Damn, that was pretty. He stroked the skin, just to feel it

now. Then, before he could decide this was unwise, he let a solid swat fly.

"Mmm." Tad twisted, looking back at him with a smile that was pure sunshine. "Thank you, Sir. More, please."

Okay, well, that was straightforward and clear as a bell, and exactly what he needed to hear. "You got it, baby."

He laid down a half-dozen blows, watching the rosy pink bloom on Tad's backside.

Tad pressed back toward him, arching, feet spreading wider. "Yes. Yes, Sir. Thank you."

Strait stared down, swallowing his groan, not sure at all if this was supposed to turn him on, or if he should worry about it because it did. He let himself stroke a little, appreciate the heat of that taut skin. "You need more, baby?"

Tad pressed against his fingers and the sound his lover made to answer his touch—a low, needy moan—had to be meant to turn him on, right?

"More, Sir. Doesn't it feel good? Go harder if you want to. Try it. I want whatever you've got."

"I want..." He wanted Tad to fly, he wanted the man to be dizzy with it, and he wanted to be the one who did it.

He reared back and popped Tad's ass nice and hard.

Tad gasped and tensed and, for a horrible moment, he thought maybe he'd gone too far. But suddenly Tad tossed that mop of blond hair, nodding for him. "Yes!" The word was breathed out with a sigh and sounded utterly satisfied. "So good, Sir."

"Damn, baby." He gave Tad two more hard strokes before letting his nails drag along that reddening skin.

He was rewarded with a long, shuddering breath, and Tad's head dropped forward, hanging from narrow shoulders. "Yours."

Lord have mercy. He leaned down and brushed the

small of Tad's back with his lips, letting his burning hand slide down his lover's thigh.

Tad moaned again, legs spreading wide, shameless. So much pale, smooth skin making the angry red marks stand out for him to admire.

He traced one mark with the tip of his tongue, then another, following the heat and knowing he would be leaving a chill behind.

Goose bumps spread across the colorful skin making Tad shiver. "Cold, Sir."

"Mmhmm. You taste hot." He patted Tad's thigh. "Burning, even."

"Burning because of you." Tad sounded far away, or high.

Suddenly he was unsure what he was supposed to do, and that wasn't a familiar feeling. He rested his cheek against Tad's ass, totally forgetting about his stubble until Tad hissed.

"Do you want me? Tell me what you want, Sir. Do you want to fuck me? Do you want my mouth? Anything you want."

Jesus Christ on a sparkly pink pogo stick. His knees damn near buckled. "I want your ass, baby."

Was that his voice—so deep and harsh?

Tad moaned for him, long and hungry. "Please. Yes, please, Sir."

"Lube." He headed for his ditty bag, which he'd stocked. Well.

His fucking cock was hard as nails, leaking and aching all the way to the root.

Tad's eyes were on him, watching him like a hawk with big, dark pupils, his lover's face flushed pink. "Want you."

"You're fixin' to have me. I want to feel you, all hot around my cock." He was on fucking fire.

He grabbed his lube and a line of condoms, losing his pants on the way back to the bed.

"So ready. Take what you want. I'll be everything you need." Tad hadn't stopped moving since he'd stepped away, rocking back, arching, lifting and dropping that blond head.

"Pretty, pretty." He slicked his fingers, and as soon as they were wet, he circled Tad's tight little hole. "Damn, baby."

"Oh god." Tad gasped and leaned into his fingers, that little pucker flexing and body begging. "Sir. Please."

He didn't play. He pressed in with two fingers, fucking Tad firmly and getting him ready while he gloved his needy cock.

Tad sighed and rode his fingers, not shy at all about needing him. Those red ass cheeks, shone hotly at him, reminding him what he'd done, how much Tad wanted it, and how they got to this moment.

He sucked in a deep breath, his entire body insisting that he give them what they needed. "You ready?"

"Yes, Sir." Tad shifted from foot to foot for a second getting balanced and then nodded. "So ready for you."

"You tell me if I go too hard." He pulled his fingers out, slicked his hard-on, and lined up.

"Yellow for slow down, red for stop, Sir. But I want to feel you on the beach tomorrow."

"You will." He didn't wait a second longer. Tad said he wanted it. Strait was fixin' to give it. He thrust in, filling that burning little hole in a single, smooth stroke.

Tad shouted a cry and stretched out on the bed, knees braced against the mattress and fingers fisting in the sheets. His lover tensed around him, clenching tight. Those muscles around his prick fluttered madly, and once his hips were touching Tad's burning skin, he stopped and stayed.

He got a whimper, and Tad forced a couple of deep breaths between rough pants, finally relaxing. "Fuck. You feel huge." Tad shuddered again but managed to loosen up some more. "Please."

"Please what, baby?" He closed his eyes and breathed, focusing on controlling his need.

"Want you, Sir. Please. Please fuck me." Tad pressed back toward him, and he sank impossibly deeper.

Shit, he could do that. He could so do that. He pulled back, almost all the way out, then he took a long breath, and rocked back in. It was easy to find a rhythm, to start fucking his baby, give Tad what he asked for.

"Yes." Tad arched into each thrust. "Hard, Sir. Like you said."

That was what he intended. He slammed in, again and again, slapping Tad's ass with his body.

Tad offered him resistance at first and tried to meet every thrust but quickly dissolved into moans and grunts. He never gave any sign it was too much, and it wasn't long before he could feel Tad trembling.

"Want you to come on my cock, baby. Want to feel it." Strait fought to get the words out, because he was damn close, but he had a responsibility to push Tad over the edge.

Tad nodded, gasped a second later, muscles spasming and locking down around him. "Sir!" Tad shouted, repeating it over and over, shaking with the release.

"Jesus!" His toes curled and he rocked forward, burying himself to the root and bucking until he shot.

Tad was breathing hard, fingers still gripping the sheets. His lover's back pressed up into his chest with every inhale.

"Baby." *Are you okay? Please be okay.*

"Mmm. Sir." Tad hummed and stretched under him like a cat ready for a nap in the sunshine.

As soon as he caught his breath, he pulled out and got them cleaned up, then he crawled up in the bed and dragged Tad into the curve of his body, making sure they could both see the ocean.

Tad threaded their fingers. "That was perfect. You're perfect. Thank you."

He kissed the back of Tad's neck, the thick shock of pale hair tickling his cheeks. "Thank you, baby. I'm glad you're here."

"I am too. I want to be where you are. Anywhere. But right here...this is like paradise."

Tad was definitely okay. Better than okay; Tad was happy.

So if he was a little confused, that worked.

11

T ad stepped out of the shower, dried off, and walked
 back into the bedroom naked. It was warm enough,
they were all alone, and his butt was nice and pink. He
decided to enjoy it a little. He felt fantastic.

Strait was still in bed, maybe sleeping, maybe dozing it
was hard to tell. He was a little smug that he hadn't
completely misread the cowboy; the man inside was a little
more than just macho after all.

He walked out onto the balcony to watch the waves and
leaned on a railing to one side of the endless pool. The view
was amazing, the quiet, the privacy...he could see why Strait
loved it here so much.

Strait was already beginning to relax. It was fascinating,
because he would have said Strait was fairly chill as it was,
but being here the little lines around his eyes had started to
fade.

After listening to the ocean for a bit and relaxing in the
sun he started to feel his shoulders warm up, and figured
he'd better find a robe or some clothes before he burned.
Strait was very serious about making sure he wore

sunscreen, and the only burn he wanted to feel right now was on his ass.

He wandered back into the bedroom and found a light robe behind one of the many doors. He felt totally spoiled as he pulled it on and wandered back to the bed. Strait's permanently tanned skin was calling his name.

"Mmm... God, it's good to be home." Strait stretched like a huge, lazy cat, muscles rippling and shifting.

"This is home, huh?" He leaned over and kissed Strait's shoulder, tasting his lover's skin. "More than your ranch?" That explained the relaxed look.

"Mmhmm. I will never leave the ranch. It's my responsibility, my family is there, and I love it, but here? This? This is my space."

"I can tell. You already look happier. Thank you for sharing your space with me." Tad slid his hand into Strait's and kissed Strait's knuckles.

"I am happy. I love lazing in the sun and inventing shit." Strait rolled over on top of him, kissing him with focus.

He melted into it, like he did all of Strait's kisses. It cast some kind of spell, made everything else disappear so his whole world was just Strait. The heavy body dragged against his, and he felt every hair, every place they rasped.

He remembered how that had felt on his ass.

But the ache in his chest was new. It started out faint, but it grew fast, and now it was undeniable. He cupped Strait's scratchy jaw and blinked his eyes open to look into those dark eyes. So deep he could get lost in them.

"Hey, baby." Strait stroked his jaw, his chin. "You good?"

"I'm so good. I just think I'm falling hard for you."

Strait nodded. "I'll make you happy, Tad. You got my word."

"I believe you. It's just amazing and new. I've never felt

like this before." He didn't mean to worry Strait, so he made sure to smile. "It's big. I don't have my head around it yet."

"You breathe, I just want you to know I got you. All the way."

He took a breath like Strait had made it an order and he exhaled, letting the butterflies go. "I know." He leaned up and took a light kiss. "And I've got you."

"Perfect." Strait bit at his chin, just nibbling. "What would you like to do today? Anything?"

"Get out on the water? Swim or kayak or something?" *And talk. We should probably talk.*

"I'm supremely easy. This place—it's where I fill myself up."

"I get it. I feel spoiled and lazy. I wouldn't want to leave either." He loved the way Strait was just hanging over him, in no hurry with nowhere to go. He felt very safe and comfortable here.

"So... I didn't hurt you last night? You're okay?" Those dark eyes were so serious.

"Yes, Sir. Look." He flipped over and wiggled his still-pink butt for Strait and grinned over his shoulder. "Pretty, right? I feel great. I'm going to feel you all day long."

"Mmm...yum." Strait rolled his hips, dragging over his ass, letting it burn.

He hissed at the sweet burn and arched his back. "You like that, huh? I didn't weird you out?"

"I was worried I'd hurt you, but you let me know it was good. That you were turned on." Tad could see the 'right?' in Strait's eyes.

"Turned on and all yours." He flipped back over so he could see Strait better, make sure they were communicating. "Like, really yours. Whatever you want kind of yours."

"Really mine." Strait looked wondering. "I want to—I need you to tell me what that means to you."

"Okay." It was time for that. He hoped Strait was ready. He gave Strait a little push to settle him back in bed and sat up enough that he could look at Strait seriously. "You want some coffee first? Maybe with some Baileys?" He was mostly joking.

"Coffee and orange juice for me, I think. Or no, pineapple juice. We should have fresh in the bar here."

"I'll get it." He slid off the bed and padded over to the bar, pleased when he found the right set of doors on the first try. "Fresh pineapple juice is such a treat. I don't think I've ever had it." He found glasses above the bar and poured some for each of them. "I feel so spoiled."

"That's the point, honey. To be spoiled." Strait rolled onto one side, watching him.

"Okay." Tad walked back over with their juice, letting Strait get an eyeful. "For you, Sir."

"Mmm... Thank you, baby. You rock." Strait's eyes dragged over his body.

He sat on the bed and rested against Strait's hip. "The bar we met in? I used to go there every Friday night. That crew cares about me, they're friends." He sipped his juice and couldn't hide the little moan as the sweet and tart flavor washed over his tongue, waking him up. "Oh. That's delicious. Amazing."

"Mmhmm. Perfect. That's good, right? That they care?" One of Strait's hands curled around his hip.

"Yes. They're good people. But there's a reason none of them, not even Rory, were more than very casual lovers." He took another sip, finding the brightness of the juice clarifying. "I spent Saturday nights at a club more...off the beaten path." Or on the beaten path, he supposed. "A kinky place with guys that wanted to play a little rougher."

He blushed, maybe because he hadn't ever told anyone but Cooper about his Saturdays, and Cooper spent a lot of time worrying. He had no idea what Strait might say.

One of Strait's eyebrows went up, a dark arch on the chiseled face. "I got to say, I don't like the idea of other men touching you like that."

Other men. He smiled, giving Strait a coy look from under his eyelashes. "Well no one has since I met you."

"That's good to know." That little growl settled in his belly. "I intend to give you what you need."

He shivered and licked his lips. That was exactly what he wanted to hear. "Thank you, *Sir*. I intend to make sure you get everything you want."

Strait reached out and rubbed his lips, dragging that thumb over his skin. "I want everything. All of you."

"Every inch. Every thought." He nuzzled into Strait's big hand and kissed the palm. It was everything he wanted. He couldn't believe it, it still felt like a fantasy or a dream in some ways. But Strait was solid and real.

"I won't ask you to give up your life, but I want you with me, as much as you can. I want to share my life with you."

"I have to work, but I can cut back a little. Will you take me into Austin sometimes on Fridays so we can hang out with Cooper and everybody?" He could show Strait off; people would love him.

"Of course, and your friends can visit at the ranch, even here, if we schedule it. I do need my time here just us, to refocus. Fair?"

Let's see. Huge ranch. Island paradise. Yacht. Dogs. Access to my friends. Totally fair.

"You're good to me." Tad leaned closer, stretching up for a kiss.

"I want to be." He got a slow, lazy smile, then a kiss that burned him to the ground.

When it ended he sat there, tingling, frozen, with his eyes closed. "Mmm. When I open my eyes, I want to be on an island paradise with the hottest man on earth." He opened them and grinned at Strait. "I got my wish!"

"Excellent. Breakfast or a nice long swim in the pool first?"

"Breakfast. You need food. And then we can float." He stood, belting his robe this time. Not that he couldn't stay in bed with Strait all day. "What are we having?"

"Mmm... I bet there's fruit salad in the fridge. I need to see what else there is. Julia and Warren will have been by early this morning."

"I love that you have people everywhere you go. I can't wait to meet them." Tad went back to the fridge and found the fruit salad. It was beautiful, so different than what he'd make back home. "Ooh. Look at this."

"I know. It's not this good anywhere else." Strait picked up a note, scanned it. "She left cherry danish for breakfast, there's ham and cheese croissants for lunch, and she left shrimp for the grill along with a salad and rice."

God, that all sounded so good. He loved a cherry danish. "Mmm. I'm going to love being here."

"I do. It's where I build up my batteries." Strait grabbed a fork and pierced a bite of pineapple. "And spend hours soaking up sunshine."

"When do I get to see the yacht? I could soak up some sun on a yacht, I bet. I'm going to ease myself into this tan beach bunny thing."

"I can call down, have them get it ready for tomorrow, if you want."

His dad had a yacht. He hadn't been invited on it in years. "Could you? I'd love that." He found and set out the danish and put on some coffee, just in case.

"Sure. I'll introduce you to the crew, too, so you can call down."

Strait had a crew. That made him smile. His burly cowboy had luxury everywhere he went. "It's funny, I was brought up with money. I'm not lacking for it now, but I've never lived like this. It feels like a fairy tale. Every time I turn around there are more people to meet."

"I feel like that. I mean, I never hurt for money, but I made a couple of inventions that ended up being the right thing at the right time."

"My lover, the inventor. It has a sexy ring to it." He waved Strait over and held up a danish for him to taste.

Strait chuckled and playfully took a bite of the pastry, growling a little as he did.

"See? Sexy." He took a bite himself. "Mm!"

They ate for a bit, sharing bites and sipping juice. There was so much he wanted to do it kind of made him anxious —so many choices. But they had all the time in the world, so he made himself take a deep breath.

"We should watch the sunset tonight. I haven't just sat and watched the sun go down in forever."

"Oh hell yes. We can sit in the pool, have a margarita, watch the sunset. That's one of my favorite moments."

There was nothing about his lover that wasn't romantic. Except the stuff that went beyond romance and set him on fire.

Tad looked around the room that opened right up onto the pool like it was outside. "So what's all the netting for?

Nighttime? Are there that many bugs? Do they bite? What if I have to get up to pee?"

"Mosquitos, moths—I like to read at night and they're drawn to the light." Strait showed him where the controls were to close the netting and the glass walls. "I tend to put the netting up at night, just so I don't have to worry about it." Strait stepped out onto the porch. "This is our beach. It goes from the line of dark rocks over there to the hibiscus hedge over that way."

"Our beach?" It was Strait's beach, but how sweet was that? He followed where Strait was pointing, taking in the wide stretch of beach. "It's beautiful. We're all alone out here."

"It is. Peace, quiet. I love it." Strait was more into his quiet time, more than anyone Tad knew.

Maybe a touch more than Tad was himself, but he could work, he could entertain himself sometimes, give Strait his space. Probably.

He leaned against Strait to soak in some of that strong, quiet peace.

"Mmm..." Strait held him, taking him over to this huge... bed. It was a bed on a swing outside. A bed. Outside. That was a swing.

"Oh my God, Strait." He turned and sat carefully on the edge, feeling it move with him. "Did you invent this too?"

"I built it. There are a couple around the house—one is a lounger, and one is a bench chair." Strait climbed in. "More fun than hammocks."

He lay down and rolled up against Strait. "Comfy. You built this? Is there anything you can't do?"

"I'm no good at art, at making things pretty. And I let the guys dress me."

"I can take that over. I'd love to dress you." He sat up on

an elbow and looked at Strait. "Not just pick out clothes, actually dress you."

"Yeah?" Strait smiled, a slow, hot expression that turned peaceful into blistering. "That's a damn pretty visual."

"Uh-huh." He felt that look like lightning, the heat running up his spine. "Yes, Sir."

"Mmm…" Strait dragged one hand down along his side, cupping his ass and squeezing.

Tad nipped at Strait's chin. "Do you bring lovers here usually?"

"No. This is my haven. I don't bring casual lovers here."

Oh, that set a fire in his belly and warmed him right up.

"I'm honored, Sir." Tad moved over Strait and kissed him, then grinned "I'll be respectful. I was taught manners once."

"Once upon a time. At some point, I need you to meet my people. They'll want to know you. Have you over."

"Right. You have people. Oh, God. Okay. I can be super extra mom-polite too… I think I remember how." Parents. Family. Nothing to be nervous about. They couldn't all be as abrasive as his own. Right?

"I have people. I am out to them, and they're all friendly. We have rainbows all over on both sides."

He laughed. "Out? I'm more worried about impressing your mother. Being out is the easy part!" Seriously. You only got one chance to make a good impression on Mom.

"She'll like you, I think. You like brisket and margaritas and dogs."

"Tell me about them. Your parents." He climbed over Strait and straddled him where he could look down and see his handsome lover's face.

"Daddy's an oil man like his daddy and his daddy before him. A cowboy. Salt of the earth. Not mean, or even undemonstrative, but he's of the earth." Strait smiled, and the look was fond. "Momma, on the other hand? She's pure air—this free-spirited, happy, goofy artist. She loves to cook and draw and she's all light."

He wondered if Strait knew that he was a good mix of both of them. Grounded in the earth, a cowboy for sure, but happy and free-spirited too. That seemed like a tough balance. No wonder Strait was so happy here but so much a part of the ranch as well. "I love how you look when you talk about them. You must love them very much."

"I love them to death. My whole family is shockingly boring and lacking drama."

"Oh, don't you worry. If you ever meet mine there will be enough drama to go around. I can't wait to meet yours. Honestly. It makes me nervous, but not like, 'I don't want to' nervous."

"Right. Normal nerves. I get that. They'll love you. They'll love that I finally found someone to introduce them to."

He slid his hands over Strait's chest. "Are you saying you've never taken anyone home either?" No pressure there, wow.

"Lots of buddies, couple of frat brothers."

Right. Frat brothers. "You'd lost one the night we met."

"Dave. He was a close friend, one of the best I'd ever had."

Tad brushed Strait's warm cheek. "More than a friend maybe?"

"We tried, but we—I don't know how to explain it without being tacky, but we didn't fit."

He shrugged. "It's not tacky to say things didn't work out. Cooper and I tried and that was...just no." He laughed. "Yeah, a big no. But we fooled around a little sometimes."

"Right. Me and Dave, we might share a guy for a night. Turn him inside out." Strait waggled his eyebrows.

Tad laughed again. "Oh, I gotcha. Sounds like fun though. I'm sorry I didn't get to meet him." It was hard to think of the guy on that barstool and the man lying here in this swinging bed with him as the same person. Strait had been in a dark place that night.

"I'm not. He would have tried to seduce you, and I would have had to kick his ass."

"Oh, you were good friends." He couldn't stop giggling. What a wonderful conversation and a great way to remember a friend.

"We were best buddies. I miss his face."

"Yeah, I can tell. He seems like someone worth thinking about. I'd thank him for putting your cowboy butt in my favorite bar if I could."

Strait hugged him with one arm. "He would have laughed and laughed. All those days of praying for my guy, and he led me right to you."

"Guess it was meant to be." He leaned down and kissed Strait. "Swim?"

"Hell yes. Let's go play in the waves. You need sunscreen?"

"When I get out. I want to be a tan bunny." He slid off the bed. "I guess I need my suit?"

"Totally up to you. My security team is exceptional. They keep the photogs away."

So casual.

My security team.

"You have security? For real? Will my bare butt scare them? Will anything mean try to bite my winky?" He gave Strait a sparkling smile.

"I have security. They have strict orders to be out of

sight, out of mind. They've seen bare butts. I have never had mine bitten, but I guarantee nothing. Run up and get your suit. I have one in the press down here."

"Okay! Save naked for the pool tonight?" He hurried back upstairs to change. Strait was so full of surprises, and he just didn't act like a man that had this kind of money. He didn't throw it around, or brag, he just lived in a way he was comfortable. He'd known people with a lot less that acted as if they had a great deal more.

Like my parents.

He wiggled his deliciously sore backside into his speedo, grabbed sunglasses, and hurried back, not wanting to keep his lover waiting.

Strait stood there in black trunks, dark glasses, and a ball cap. Music was playing on the speakers, and he was swaying, muscles rippling.

"Jesus, could you be any hotter right now?" Tad put his shades on and slipped up against Strait to dance with him.

"Hmm... I was just waiting for you, honey." One solid hand landed on his ass.

"Do we need towels?" He swayed with Strait, arching into that big hand. "Tell me where."

"In the press over there." The big cabinet had drawers and a place where towels hung.

Okay, that was cool.

"Wow. I'll tell you what, you can travel back to the ranch. I'll just be your island boy toy." He pulled out two towels.

"You'd miss me and the dogs." Strait didn't sound worried.

"Oh, Bart would miss his swimming buddy, huh? I guess I'll have to go back with you." He slipped a hand into Strait's. "Beach?"

"Beach. Where's your favorite place to vacation, honey?" They wandered down on the warm, white sand.

"Here. Right here." He laughed, loving the soft sand in his toes. "What's better than this?"

"I have no idea, but this is my fantasy. I wanted to make sure yours matches."

"Baby, if you're in it, it matches. But this is paradise for sure. I love the beach. I'm in love with this beach." He let go of Strait's hand as they neared the water and dropped their towels where they'd stay dry.

"Our beach." Strait wandered in, just fearless and easy. The water lapped at his shins for a long while, and then Strait was up to his waist.

He followed easily, confident about water. It was warmer than he'd expected, clearer, and he waded in alongside Strait, the water hitting his ribcage. "How far out do you swim?"

"Alone, I go out to the next shelf. I went out too far once, and the guys had to come get me. It *sucked*."

"Scary. Is there a bad current?" He took a few more steps, went under for a second to soak his hair and popped up again to float.

"I didn't think so, but suddenly I was far out and tired, and I couldn't make it back." Strait rolled his eyes. "I learned my limits there."

"Don't worry, cowboy. Your secret is safe with me." Tad floated, circling his arms to pull himself farther out. "No diving board."

"No. And the infinity pool isn't deep enough. Sorry." Strait stretched out and floated, body relaxed and limp.

"I'll live." God, so pretty. He dove under Strait and pinched his butt.

Strait piked down and immediately came after him,

playing with him, chasing and touching him. It felt amazing, the way Strait focused on him, wanted to be, literally, hands-on.

He giggled and swam away. He was a good swimmer, but Strait was bigger and faster—one of the very best things about his lover—and just plain played dirty. Strait got ahold of his foot and tugged them close together. "Hey! Is that cheating? I think that might be cheating."

"All's fair, honey." Then Strait kissed him, tongue pressing in like they were both starving.

He moaned and wrapped his legs around Strait's middle, kissing back, opening so Strait could have his fill. If there was such a thing. He hadn't yet, he hoped he never would.

"Mmm...how's your pretty butt, honey? Not sore?"

"It's cooler in the water for sure." He grinned, maybe a little smugly. "I like it a little sore."

"I liked it, but I'm glad I didn't hurt you." Strait squeezed his ass a little harder.

Strait had the best hands. "I thought you would. You just had to believe you could play a little rough. That I wouldn't break. And I won't." It was his turn to take a kiss, and when he pulled away, he dragged his teeth along his cowboy's lower lip.

"Toothy!" Strait chuckled but let him swim away before catching him again.

He yelped and splashed. "Is that a mer-cowboy after me?"

"Yee-haw glub glub?" Strait was melted, happy, and right here with him in paradise.

"So what do you want to do with me tonight, Sir?" He purred and slipped a hand under the waistband of Strait's trunks. "Tie me up? Pin me down? I can be very bad."

"Can you? Are you wicked?" Strait hummed under his breath. "I'm new to this, honey, but I'll figure it out."

"Don't think so hard, cowboy. Just...feel." He curled his fingers around Strait's perfect cock and stroked slowly. "And take what you want. Anything you want."

Strait's eyelids got heavy, and his lips parted. "I want to make all your dreams come true. Every one."

"Let's start with this one. You and me, alone on a beach, broad daylight, no one watching me get you off but the fish."

"Mmm..." Strait cupped the back of his head, kissing him deep enough that he almost lost the thread, his rhythm hiccupping.

Tad tried to concentrate, but melted into Strait, so ready to give him anything he wanted. Strait groaned for him, dragging him up against that perfect, flat belly.

He worked the head of Strait's cock with his thumb, circling and driving through the slit again and again, letting Strait hold him up as the water lapped at them.

Strait groaned, nipping his lip. "Steady, honey. Make it last."

"Yes, Sir. I can do that." Fuck, that was so hot. He drew it out, longer strokes, feeling every vein under his fingers. "Just how you want it."

"Good deal. I want to be able to last tonight. I want to tear your pretty ass up."

He gasped, he couldn't help it. Tad wanted that too. He'd take it right now. "I love it when you talk like that."

Strait nuzzled his temple. "I love the sight of your ass, hot and pink, hole wrapped around my cock."

"You're making me ache, Sir. You're going to make me wait all day for you?" The thought was wonderful and awful. Perfect.

"You able to do that for me, baby? Can you give me that?"

He nodded, feeling strangely breathless. "I can. I will give you whatever you want."

"Then hold on for me, and I swear to God, I'll make it worth it for you tonight."

Tad stretched up and nipped at Strait's chin. "Yes, Sir. I can't wait."

"Mmm...well, you can, for a bit." Strait winked at him, then took his mouth again.

Jesus, was it dinner time yet? He wiggled free. "You cheated. Again." He laughed and swam out of reach.

"Me? You sure it was me?" Strait stretched up tall, exposing that beautiful hard-on.

"Yes. And now you're just showing off. I really like it, you look like my own personal sun god, but you're totally showing off." He flipped over in the water and gave Strait a look at his still-pink backside.

The smack was surprising, because he could barely hear it, but he felt it.

He yelped in surprise and rolled over again giving Strait a wide-eyed stare. "Sir!"

Strait blinked back. "Too hard?"

He gave Strait a coy smile. "No, Sir. You just surprised me." And how fun was that?

"Surprise isn't against the rules." Strait reeled him in.

"I guess you'd know, since they're your rules. Mostly." He loved how Strait was relaxing into this.

"No, I think the real rules, those need to be ours. Yours and mine."

"Oh. Yes." He looked up and slid a wet hand over Strait's warm cheek. "Mr. Strait. I think you should kiss me before we have a talk about the rules."

"I think that's a damn fine idea." Strait pulled him in close, rubbing them together as he got the kiss he wanted.

"Mm." He soaked Strait in, but he was a little distracted by the idea of actual rules. He'd never lived this before; he'd always agreed on rules for an evening, not for forever.

Strait was so—focused; those eyes never left his, never stopped gazing into him.

"You'll laugh at me. I don't really know how to make rules." He tried to give that focus back to Strait though. At least so Strait would see he was being honest.

"Me either. So we'll have a ball figuring that out. I won't harm you, though. You're precious to me."

"I know you won't. I trust you. Completely. I love you." He wasn't nervous about that anymore, he was just...awed. Happy.

"I love you, honey. I swear to God, I'm going to make you happy."

"Well, fortunately for you, you don't have to try very hard. I already am." Tad laughed and took Strait's hand, leading him back toward the beach.

"Are you ready to explore the wonders of the outside shower?" Strait cupped his butt and squeezed.

"Yes." He leaned into the touch. "Too bad I can't explore you while we're at it."

"Ah, it's walled on two sides and the house protects you on the other. We can explore all we want."

He snorted. "Sure. Explore. But that's it. So mean." He grinned though, he liked Strait's game, if that's what it was. He liked the idea of keeping each other running all day.

"That's me. The meanest. Mr. Mean." Strait's chuckle was absolutely wicked.

He let Strait lead him into the shower, fantasizing about what he could do—one day—to his big, hot lover under the blue sky and sunshine. Maybe he could make Strait scream loud enough to freak out the security guys.

The outdoor shower was the size of three of his bathrooms, and someone had put out pineapple juice and towels.

"This is not a shower, Strait. It's not your usual rustic, beachy, get the sand off affair at all. This is a spa. I mean... juice? Are you kidding me? Where did you take me? You can't seriously live here." He grinned, because of course Strait could, but even growing up with money, he'd never seen anything like this place. Part of him wanted to take pictures and rub his father's nose in them.

"Only a chunk of the year. I always spend the spring at the ranch, no matter what." Strait sucked down his juice. "And Christmas. I spend Christmas with my folks."

"Ugh. Christmas." Not his favorite holiday. But Strait obviously liked it so he didn't say that. "You go every year?"

"Well, we get together every year. Sometimes we go to Colorado or Jackson Hole. One time we went to the Swiss Alps. The important part was that we are all together."

"That sounds nice." He slipped out of his suit so he could rinse it off. "I don't have Christmas plans."

"Well, you do now." Strait scooped him up and kissed him, turning on the water. "We'll celebrate until you're rosy."

"Like Rudolph's nose?" He never understood what it meant to swoon until Strait kissed him.

"You can lead me through the fog." Strait's laughter tickled his lips. "Ho ho ho."

"Mm. I'm only a ho for you, Santa." He nipped at Strait's lip.

Strait snorted, cradling the back of his head and tilting him.

He threw his arms around Strait's neck and laughed, admiring the way the sun lit his man up. "Don't drop me, Sir!"

"Never, baby. Not on your life." Strait nibbled his collarbone, teasing his skin.

"Mm." He sighed and dropped his head back, almost dead weight in Strait's arms and loving every second of this. He was going to be a mess by tonight.

"You taste like the sea." Strait hoisted him up and bit one nipple.

"Sir!" He shouted, not caring if anyone heard him. This was Strait's place. "No fair." His moan was quieter, and he shoved a hand into Strait's hair.

He felt the wicked smile that curved against his chest, then he got another bite, another soft suck.

He moaned and just enjoyed it, as if he had another choice. Fuck him. He'd created—or let loose—a wicked and wonderful monster.

Strait moaned, working his one nip until he needed to scream, just throw his head back and let loose.

"Strait! Sir... Sir." He tried to arch, to find a little friction for his poor neglected prick but he didn't find any, not the way Strait was holding him.

"Mmhmm?" That little vibration was enough to drive him mad.

"Fuck. Why don't we...uh. Go watch a movie?" No, that was a bad idea. Too private, too much time for Strait to get handsy. "No. Go for a walk? Want...to?" He grunted in frustration when his skin broke out in goose bumps, like his body was betraying him. "A walk. Right? Wouldn't that be nice?"

"You want a walk, baby? With this other little nipple begging attention?"

"It's not begging. I'm not begging. I mean, I am a little because you're making me crazy, Strait. And I'm trying to be good and wait for you, but—" Tad blinked and bit his lips together to shut himself up.

"Mmm... You are delicious." Strait found his other nip and started sucking hard.

He gasped and squeezed his eyes shut so hard he forced tears out of the corners. He snaked a hand down between them, he just needed something, a little touch, it wasn't a big deal. But he ached like he might explode, and Strait wasn't giving him anything. How was that fair?

Strait swatted his hand away, biting hard. "No."

He yanked his hand back and whimpered at the sting. "Please?"

"No, baby. We agreed. We're going to wait, then you're going to come on my cock, and it's going to be so good."

Fuck. "Fine." He'd level the playing field. He reached for Strait's cock instead. If Strait didn't want to play fair, he could be a naughty boy.

"You are." Strait chuckled, letting him touch, letting him feel that long, proud cock.

It was gorgeous and heavy in his hand, and he stroked it lazily, but it wasn't even the most amazing thing about Strait and that just made him tingly all over. Strait ticked off boxes for him he hadn't even known he had.

"I am going to have you ride me tonight, baby, take my cock all the way to the root." Strait's voice was like gravel.

God, it was all he could do not to groan. "Yes, Sir. I'll drive you out of your mind."

"I would expect nothing less from you." There was a sure heat, like Strait believed in this, in him, and wasn't that fucking wild?

Tad managed to wiggle free—or Strait let him wiggle

free—and he grabbed the shampoo. "We're wasting water." He winked and got Strait's hair wet, then worked the shampoo in. Even Strait's shampoo smelled like the beach. The place was amazing.

"Mmm... You have good hands, baby."

"They love your body, that's all." And he liked to touch.

"Good. Don't stop." That pirate smile glinted at him, wicked and blistering.

"No, Sir. I won't." He liked that smile; he thought maybe Strait reserved that look just for him. He scrubbed and rinsed Strait's hair, then started massaging his cowboy's muscles with soapy fingers, glad to have the focus back on Strait so he could tell his body to calm down and chill out. It was going to be hours before he got what he needed—what they both needed.

Strait's nipples were hard and stiff, the tips teasing his palms and he rubbed circles.

He licked his lips. Who was he kidding? This was not taking his mind off anything. Strait was hot as the sun, and the sun was pretty damn hot here. He rinsed the soap off Strait's chest and teased one lovely little bud with his tongue.

"Mmm..." Strait tilted his face up, kissing him like there was nothing else on earth he'd rather do.

He nipped at Strait's tongue and lower lip playfully. "Stop that." Tad reached around and shut the water off. "Put a towel on. You're too tempting. Way too tempting."

"That's me. Too tempting." Strait chuckled low, then dragged him close. "You don't want to dry me off?"

"Yes. No. Dammit. Yes." He snatched a towel and dragged it over Strait's damp shoulders.

"Mmm... I love how you smell. You make me hungry."

"There's lots of fruit in the fridge..." Tad tucked the towel around Strait's hips.

"Mmhmm. Lots. Come feed me?"

You're killing me, baby. He dried off and wrapped a towel around himself too. "Yes, Sir."

"My good boy." Strait drew him in, one hand sliding down to cup his ass.

"Oh." He felt those words in his spine—in his skin, in his balls. That's what he was, what he wanted to be for Strait. He went up on his toes, asking for a kiss. "That's me."

"Hell, yes." Strait leaned down, the long, slow connection everything he asked for.

Strait's good boy. That thought made this easier. He could buzz all day, he could want Strait so badly, he could get close to losing his mind because it was for Strait. It was what Strait asked him to do.

He relaxed into the kiss, every nerve burning for his Master.

12

By the time they were done with supper, Strait was aching he was so hard, and Tad was obviously getting grumpy. He wanted to ask if this was right, if this was what Tad wanted, but he couldn't figure out how without losing the game.

He'd be damned if he didn't get this right for his lover.

"I've been thinking about you all day." Tad slid up next to him, a hot hand landing on his belly. "Which I know is the point, and fuck, Sir, it's working."

"Mmm... Your hand is like a brand." He wrapped one hand around Tad's ass, dragging him in closer. Pretty baby—Strait decided that he liked need on Tad's face.

"You could have more than my hand," Tad offered, so obviously trying to seduce him.

"I can." It wasn't a question. "You know how long it's been since I felt your mouth around my cock?"

He wanted to feel Tad—mouth, hand, ass—all around him.

Tad's pupils grew into dark pools, and the hand on his

belly slid lower to rub him through his shorts. "Let me fix that. Right now."

"Show me what you got, baby. I want to watch you suck me." In fact he thought this was a delicious idea.

"Yes, please." Tad sank to his knees right there and tugged his shorts down. "Oh, man. This is for me?" Tad circled his fingers around the base and kissed the very tip of his cock.

"Mmhmm. All yours. Every goddamn inch." And he wanted to see Tad work it all.

"Thank you, Sir." Tad's tone was playful, but the tongue that bathed him balls to tip wasn't.

Oh, now he could learn to live with that. He leaned back, his thighs going taut. "Good boy."

Tad hummed, around the head of his cock, then the rest of his length was surrounded in wet heat as the blond head began to bob slowly in his lap.

He brushed his fingers through the heavy strands, not pushing, but not-not pushing. He wasn't going to force, but he was absolutely encouraging.

Tad teased on every upstroke, lapping at the head or driving his tongue through his slit, deep enough that he felt it. A hot hand worked in tandem, stroking him between swallows.

Oh fuck him, he was going to lose it, and he wasn't ready, not quite yet. But damn, it was good. "Baby," Strait moaned, arching with the pressure in his balls.

"Mmm." Tad hummed around him until he couldn't anymore, and Strait's cock slipped deep into his throat as wicked fingers slid behind his balls, gliding over sensitive skin to tap at his hole.

He gasped out a scant warning before it was all over but the moaning, his bones rattling with the force of it.

Tad barely lasted another minute before he stood up, breathing heavily, and stared at him with wild, burning eyes. "Sir! Sir, I need... Please."

"Come here, baby." He grabbed Tad and spun him, dragging the loose, gauzy pants down and sitting Tad on his lap to face the glass where their reflection was clear as day. "Look at how beautiful you are."

Then he grabbed that sweet prick and started jacking, firm and steady strokes, using the leaking drops to ease the way.

"I... I...oh, fuck!" Tad's eyes were glued to their reflection, fingers digging into his thighs, and it didn't take but a handful of strokes to get him off. His boy shouted and moaned, babbling as he shot. "Thank you. Fuck. Thank you, Sir."

"My pretty baby." He bit down almost gently at the curve where neck and shoulder met.

Tad arched his neck, offering more, chest rising and falling as he caught his breath. "Yours, Sir. Your baby. Your boy. You're so fucking perfect."

"Mine. Damn, baby. You make me fucking happy." Strait held Tad, letting them float back down before they headed into round two. Because there was no question there was fixin' to be a round two after a while.

13

S trait had gotten the idea for a new coupling and he'd gone to his studio, starting with sketches and moving to 3D printed mockups in short order. Warren assured him that Julia was feeding his lover and changing the sheets, and that there was no shortage of pineapple on the island.

All in all, it worked out.

Julia almost never bothered him when he was working, but he knew the light tap on the door as soon as he heard it. Warren's knock was forceful, as if Warren's question was important. Julia's knock seemed more like a non-urgent intrusion.

"Come on in. I'm decent." He needed a shower and a nap, but he had shorts on.

Julie opened the door but didn't come in. She looked island breezy in bright sundress and sandals. "I'm sorry to bother you, Mr. McMasters, but Mr. Dawson asked me to ask you if you would be joining him for dinner tonight."

"Hey, you. I guess I ought to. I been in here a day or so, huh?" He could get a little lost in his workshop when an idea grabbed him. "Sure enough. If you see him, tell him he's welcome to come on up."

"It's a beautiful day." Julie came in finally, crossing to a set of French doors to open them. "A little air will help. And a clean shirt." She smiled and set a shirt on his chair. He hadn't even noticed it over her arm. "I'll pass on your invitation to Mr. Dawson."

"Yeah. Please do. I just want to tweak this little bit, but —" It was a gorgeous day out there.

"Fish and a citrus rice salad for dinner." Julie left, the door closing quietly behind her.

The next knock had to be Tad. That was fast; it couldn't have been five minutes. "Strait? Sir?"

"Hey, baby. Come on in." He stripped off his shirt and tossed it. "You want to see what I've been working on?"

Tad wandered in, looking tanned and a little beach-wild. "Uh. Sure."

"I'm working on a coupling for underwater, high-pressure..." Oh, damn. Tad smelled so good. He reached out, one hand sliding around Tad's waist.

"Sounds complicated." Tad's eyes scanned his desk. "No wonder it's taken you three days."

Three days. Huh. "Has it been so long? I need to see the sun a little."

"Yeah. The sun." Tad looked out the doors at the beach. "And me."

"And you." Someone needed him more than the coupling did. "You're always welcome up here, you know. I can get lost in the designs. It's a little like a drug."

"I don't want to disturb your work, but..." Tad sighed. "No, actually, I kind of do. I've been knocking around this place alone long enough."

He wasn't used to having to think about someone else,

about having someone here who didn't know that this happened. Inspiration was a stone-cold bitch. "You can always pop in, poke me."

"Okay." Tad slipped out of his arms. "Or you could maybe come to bed. Or dinner. That closed door spoke pretty loudly to me."

"It wasn't intended to. I had no idea the idea would turn into something." He wasn't going to feel bad because he worked. He came here to recharge, to rest, and sometimes, when he was lucky, he had an idea that came on him.

Tad's head tilted slightly. "You didn't tell me about this part. I didn't know you worked on vacation. I didn't know there was even a chance you'd just not come to bed one night. Or two. Or that I'd be sitting across from an empty seat at dinner. How did I know you weren't mad or that I hadn't..." Tad sighed.

His immediate reaction was to snarl and bite, because dammit, he was tired, and what he did was important, and he would give Tad anything he asked for. He stopped himself, closed his eyes for half a second. "I'm going to try and not be grumpy, but I'm tired, so I might sound that way. If you need me, if you need to know something, you can ask. I'll tell you the truth. You never have to wonder if I'm mad. I'll just say so."

"Okay. I need you. I need you to be at dinner tonight. I need you to sleep in our bed. I need to not be alone anymore. What I really needed was for you to tell me all of this before you disappeared."

"I didn't know I was going to get an idea. Hell, I don't bring people here, as a rule. I didn't know to warn you." He bit the words out through a building headache. "I will be at supper tonight, though. And I will be in bed. Hell, I'm exhausted. I could be in bed for a nap right now."

"Looking forward to dinner." Tad stepped close again and kissed his cheek. "Grumpy."

He got a good look at Tad's ass in tight shorts as his lover left his office.

Strait sighed and headed downstairs, stumbling on the last few steps on the way to grab a bite of pineapple and a bottle of water. He stood there, leaning on the counter trying to figure out which end was up.

"Hey." Tad was at his side in a second. "You think you'll actually make it through dinner?" Tad was watching him now, worrying. "You look exhausted. Can you take a break now? Let me be your drug for a while?"

He held out his hand, twined their fingers together. "I think that sounds amazing. You interested in sharing a shower with me?"

"Whatever you want. I...really do miss you. A little bit." Tad squeezed his fingers, eyes glued to him as he got up.

"Just a little bit?" He led Tad down a floor. "I get lost in that room. I get lost in my head. You need me, you come fetch me up."

"Okay. This is a beautiful place but it's pretty lonely without you around." Tad followed easily. "Julie said you sometimes disappear in there for days and days... I just...we probably should have talked about that so I was ready for it, you know? I was sort of shocked that first night. She said she doesn't even knock unless she has to."

"We should have talked. I come here to relax and, sometimes, when I do, I start to get ideas. It's my thing." Poor baby. It was quiet out here, and he was used to it. "I'm sorry, baby. I should have thought."

Tad leaned in and dropped his head on Strait's shoulder. "You're not used to having anyone here. I know. It's new. I'm new."

"You are, but you are my lover, my heart, and I want to do right by you. Tell you what. This gizmo makes a million, I'll take you anywhere on earth you want to go."

"Anywhere, huh?" Tad laughed. "We can spend it at the ranch. On puppies and margaritas."

"Mmm... Puppies and tequila." He stripped down, turning on the water. "Oh, this is going to feel good, baby."

"You're going to smell so much better." Tad gave him a playful smile and started tugging off his clothes. Underneath Tad's skin was already turning bronze, the pale skin was gone and there was only a hint of pink sunburn here and there. He must have spent these last few days soaking up the sun.

"Aren't you pretty?" He hummed softly, licking his lips. Oh, he could tear that sweet ass up. "My sun worshipper."

"The sun feels good. It feels healthy." Tad put a hand on his chest. "Sir."

"Mmm...baby." He wasn't sure whether or not he could ask for a little TLC. He wanted to feel good, to be spoiled some.

Tad pushed him under the water. "I feel like I haven't touched you in ages." Tad's fingers spread out over his chest and drew down toward his hips. "Don't you get sore, working like that?"

"You know it. There's not a bit of me that isn't aching." Strait leaned into the water and the touch at the same time.

"Mm. Well, we can't have that, Sir." Tad turned him gently to get to his back, and started working practiced hands into his muscles, fingers sliding easily under the spray from the shower.

"Oh..." Right. He had a lover, a beautiful boy right here that wanted to love up on him. "Don't stop."

"No, Sir. You have knots all over." He could hear the

smile in Tad's voice and knew Tad was as happy to give as he was to receive. Tad took his time finding hot spots and working them loose, and every so often dropping kisses in his back or smoothing a hand down his arm.

"Oh damn..." He couldn't decide if he wanted a nap or an orgasm more. His entire body felt boneless and loose.

Tad also washed his hair and gave him a good scrub, finally shutting the water off and handing him a towel. "Somebody needs to lie down. Then I can do a much better job on your shoulders. You're so tall."

He wrapped the towel around himself, then bent forward to take a kiss, luxuriating in it for a minute. Jesus, that was what he needed.

"Mmm." Tad melted right into him, molding to his body and holding on tight as they indulged in the kiss together.

"Come to bed, baby. I want more of your touch." He walked them to the bedroom, the wind blowing and making the sheets flutter. "Looks like a storm is coming in."

Tad seemed shocked and stayed close as they went inside. "Wow. That blew in fast. I didn't see it coming."

He looked at the clouds. They'd get rain and wind, but nothing dangerous. "They call it a squall, I think. I like the storms off the water. Are you okay with storms?"

"I think so? It's been a while since I've been in an ocean storm." Tad's eyes were watching the sky, darting from cloud to cloud. "I remember liking the wind."

"Well, we can go downstairs, if you want." He wasn't unwilling to accommodate.

"I can feel the wind here. Let's watch it from bed." Tad climbed into the sheets and patted the pillows. "We can go down and have dinner after it blows over."

"Mmm...sounds good." He dragged one hand over Tad's

hair after he settled. God, he was tired, and this was so comfortable, right here.

"Do you like storms?" Tad coaxed him to roll over onto his stomach. "Do they happen a lot here?"

"I do. I like them just fine in here. Out on an oil rig? Not so much. That's stressful. Inside and watching is just peaceful."

Tad knelt up by his shoulders and started rubbing. "Oh. No, I don't think I'd want to go out to a rig period, never mind during a storm. That sounds terrifying."

"I'm not well-suited to it, but my daddy insisted, so I did it." For six summers in a row doing scut work. It had been miserable, but he understood why Daddy had done it.

"Damn, I'm glad my parents aren't into oil." Tad laughed softly, working on his shoulders and his neck. "How does this feel?"

"Like someone loves me." And that was the god's honest truth.

"I do." Tad stretched out next to him, lying in the pillows to look at him. "I want you to work. I want you to imagine and make your amazing things. But you really disappear. I didn't know when to worry. And I know it's a flaw but I'm not very good at the solitude thing."

That was a problem, because he came here for the quiet and the solitude. Still, it was love, and he knew from his folks that ninety-nine percent of loving someone was learning to work together and compromise.

"Well, then I guess I'm just going to have to figure shit out." But honestly, his brain was sputtering like a candle drowning in wax.

"We will. Thank you for listening." Tad snuggled closer and kissed his forehead. "I do love you."

"I love you." His eyelids kept closing on him. "We'll figure it. I swear to god."

"There are worse things than feeling lonely for a couple of days in paradise. Sleep. I'm going stay right here and nap with you." Tad's arm slid over his shoulders protectively.

"Good. Good boy." *We'll dream together.*

———

IT WAS A GORGEOUS EVENING, warm and still, the squall blown over, and Julie suggested they eat outdoors. Tad liked that idea, it was different, romantic in a way. He took the silverware and two wine glasses from Julie as she headed outside.

"I can do that."

"Are you sure, Mr. Dawson?"

"I am. And I'm also sure you should call me Tad, please. Mr. Dawson makes me sound too old." Like his dad. Ugh.

"All right, Mr—Tad."

"Close! You'll get it." Tad laughed and she smiled at him and went back inside. He went out to set the table.

He'll come Tad assured himself as he set out the wine glasses. *He'll be here. He promised.* It was hard not to doubt, and he was feeling pretty salty anyway. He wanted Strait's full attention, special attention. He needed it, and he planned to get it one way or another.

"Did I miss supper? I set an alarm..." Strait's voice floated out from the dining room.

He let out a long breath, face flushing a little with relief and also with some embarrassment that he'd doubted his lover. "Out here, Sir!"

"Oh. Hey." Strait was barefoot, dressed in jeans and an

open white button-down that he was beginning to button up.

"Ooh." Tad stuck his finger out and poked Strait in the center of his chest, playing, getting in the way. "Stop there. That's enough buttons."

"You think so, do you?" He got a warm, quirky little half grin.

"I do." He flirted, giving Strait doe eyes. "This was Julie's idea. Eating out here."

"It's a gorgeous evening. That storm blew all the cobwebs away." Strait looked out over the ocean with a smile.

"It is." He moved back to the table. Strait was so handsome, standing there breathing in the beautiful night. He should have told Julie no. He knew it was petty, but he wanted his lover's attention for himself. He wanted that smile on him.

He needed to feel like Strait missed him.

"You're far away, baby." Strait turned and leaned against the porch column. "The table looks great. So do you."

That was better. "Thank you. And I'm not far away. I'm right here. Still. I've been right here." He pulled out a chair and sat, then poured himself a little of the wine Julie had left in an ice bucket.

Strait nodded and turned on some music before coming to sit down. As soon as Strait sat, Julie brought their plates.

"Thank you, lady. Go ahead on home. I can put the plates in the dishwasher." Strait winked at her, and she poured Strait's wine before kissing his cheek and waving to them.

"Night, Julie! Thank you for keeping me company!" He gave her a big smile and waggled his fingers at her as she left. He didn't miss the little shake of her head.

Strait lifted his glass, the candlelight shining in his dark eyes. "Cheers."

He looked right into them, trying like always to see how deep they went. "Cheers," he said, holding his glass out toward Strait.

Strait held his gaze, looking into him as their glasses clinked. "What do you want to bet it's fish?"

"Well, let's see. It's been fish every night so far, right?" He laughed. "So unless you requested pasta or vegetarian..."

"Nope. I didn't request anything. I'm craving a pizza though man, I have to tell you."

Tad laughed. "I feel so healthy it's disgusting." He pulled the cover off his plate. "Oh my gosh! It's fish!"

Strait gasped, the look enough to crack him up. "O. M. G!"

Then the warm, sensual laughter filled the air, wrapping around him.

He took Strait's plate cover away too and set them on the ground near the wine. Then he forked up a bite and offered it to his lover. "Maybe it will be more interesting off my fork."

Strait hummed softly, leaning forward to steal a bite. "It's good. Better off your fork." Then Strait scooted back a little bit. "Let me see if it tastes better when you're sitting on my lap."

"Hm. I don't know. Do you deserve me in your lap?" Tad got up and sauntered around the table.

"You tell me, baby. You're calling the shots right now." Strait held his gaze—the expression serious, but not ugly. "I'll give you through supper to punish me; that's your freebie."

Well, that was straightforward. "My freebie? And what

happens after that?" He climbed into Strait's lap, not the least bit deterred.

"Then I'm going to explain to your pretty little backside how the cow ate the cabbage." Strait wrapped one arm around his waist. "Remember, I learn quick."

Fuck, that was tempting, wasn't it? "You do learn fast. Or you just needed someone to give your true nature permission to breathe."

"Six of one, half-dozen of another. Do you want a bite?" Strait's eyes glinted at him. "Of fish?"

"Yes, please. I'm...hungry." He licked his lips slowly and opened his mouth. He'd been given dinner to be naughty and he planned to use it.

Strait fed him a carefully chosen bite, and Tad had to admit, it was lovely—lemony and bright. It was still fish, but it tasted good.

"Mm. I really can't complain about fish when it's this yummy. Julie is such a good cook. She taught me how to make this pineapple shrimp thing while you were locked in your office. We had it for dinner. It was so good."

"You'll have to make it for me." Strait took a bite. "And the door wasn't locked."

He made a goofy face at Strait. He didn't want to fight. "I was afraid that if you didn't want to come to bed, then you didn't want me knocking either." He put a finger over Strait's lips before the cowboy could answer. "I know. I get it now. But that was how I felt at the time."

"I'm sorry, baby. I never meant to hurt your feelings."

Oh. Oh, that was just offered over without drama, like Strait meant it.

He nodded. It was okay, now that he knew what Strait was up to. He wasn't sure yet what was going to happen the next time, but tonight wasn't for figuring that out.

Rather than drawing out the conversation, he kissed Strait instead, slow and sweet, just so Strait knew they were good. He might still decide to be naughty, but they were good.

Strait winked at him as they separated, and then fed him another bite. "You have a few bites left."

He chewed, enjoying as much as he had the first one. "I better take advantage of them, huh? Even if I do love a good cabbage story."

"I intend that you remember this one every time you sit for a couple of days."

Holy fuck. He should have said, "Yes, Sir," but he didn't. He still had a little of his freebie left, so he looked Strait right in the eye, gave his lover a knowing smile, and said, "Do you, really?"

"I do, baby. Really." Jesus, when Strait looked at him like that, like he was the only thing in the world, it made Tad melt inside. The low, honey-over-gravel voice didn't hurt either.

His cheeks were burning right along with the rest of him. "I need you," he admitted. "I need this so bad."

One hand dragged up his back, loving on him, almost petting. "I hear you, all the way. I'm going to give you what you need. You got my word. Finish your supper."

"You too." He picked up Strait's fork and held out another bite. "So, are you going to be a famous inventor again?"

"I think so, yes." Strait's eyes lit up. "I know that it didn't seem like anything important, but in the oil industry? This could be a game changer, and we have the corporation to market it, so..."

"So." Tad rubbed noses with his brilliant cowboy. "I get to be even more proud of you than I already am."

"And when it makes its first million, we'll go on a wild honeymoon."

"See the northern lights in a glass-roofed cabin in Norway or something."

Strait smiled at him, the look fond, happy. "Oh, that sounds like a plan. How does a month sound?"

Tad squinted at Strait. "You think it's going to make a million in a month? Or you think we should go on—"

Wait. Whoa. What?

"You...you said honeymoon." He had, right? Wild honeymoon. Tad's heart started pounding.

"I said honeymoon, baby." Strait lifted one hand to his lips, kissed his knuckles. That dark gaze never wavered. "Wanna?"

"You bet I wanna!" He tossed his arms around Strait's neck and hugged him, laughing. He couldn't help it; he'd never been happier in his whole life.

Strait held him close. "I love you, baby. I want you with me, forever. Side by side."

"I love you. You're my cowboy, my lover, my Dom. You're my everything." Their first and only ever argument ended with a proposal? His freebie was definitely over. "Forever. Side by side, missionary, doggie style...all of it."

Strait chuckled softly. "Mmm... I think we'll start with over my lap. I woke up dreaming of that, so obviously it's what we need, hmm?"

"Well, obviously." He loved that "we." That's what *we* need. He was fucking getting married in a month. "Right here? Or upstairs? Sir?"

"Right here, sweet baby. This is a lovely place to start. The breeze will feel amazing on your backside."

He slipped off Strait's lap, still holding that gaze, so turned on by Strait's sure, steady tone, and the little husky rumble underneath it. He tugged his shirt off, then shimmied out of his shorts. The breeze was cool on his hot skin, but that wasn't what made him shiver.

Strait scooted his chair back, spreading his legs a bit. Then he patted his thighs. "Come here, baby boy."

It wasn't a request.

"Yes, Sir." Strait had to see the way his cock totally betrayed him, stretching long and curving up toward his belly. He didn't even try to swallow his moan. He took a couple of steps closer and settled himself across Strait's wide lap, curling one arm under a strong thigh for balance.

"Mmm...pretty." Strait's hand rubbed in a gentle circle, the heat a real, actual promise. "Pretty and mine, yes?"

The "yes" came with a sharp, firm swat.

"Yes!" He lifted his head, happily surprised by the blow and by the man who dealt it. "Yes, Sir."

"Good boy. And if you need me, you're coming to see me, yes?" Another firm swat that rocked him.

"I'll knock on your door. Yes, Sir." The sting and the heat spread slowly over his ass, sinking into muscle and skin.

"Because I will tell you if I can't give you what you need." *Swat.* "And I fully intend." *Swat.* "To give you what you need." *Swat.*

"So far, so good. Oh..." That last one rocked his cock into Strait's thigh, and he wanted to hump it like a naughty puppy. He groaned softly instead as his brain tried to short out. "Or. Sir. I mean, yes, Sir. Thank you, Sir."

"Good boy. I want you to remember this when you're lonely. I'm right here." Then Strait began to pepper his ass, the rhythm steady and strong, but not bruising, not unbearable. Not punishment. This was meant to heat him up and make him burn.

He nodded, melting into his Dom, his cowboy. Drooping

heavily, almost boneless over Strait's thighs. "Right here. I love you. I'll remember, Sir. Thank you." The words were true, but he was babbling, aching, eyes crossing as he snuck a little friction for his needy prick. "I want you. Please, Sir." Strait was everything. He needed everything.

"Mmm... Sweet baby." The blows slowed, gentled. "Tell me what you need."

He knew the sound he made was basically a whimper, but he didn't know how to ask. "I need you, Sir, I need to feel you...deep."

"Mmm..." Strait stood him up, balancing him on his feet. "Go get some lube and slick yourself for me. I want you to ride me. I'll meet you on the sofa inside."

Oh. That sounded perfect. But he had to walk first. He took a couple of wobbly steps with Strait right there to steady him and then he managed to move away despite the woozy head and the baby foal legs.

He made it up the stairs to grab supplies, then hurried back to the big open living room and to his lover. He didn't want to keep Strait waiting. "Got it. I didn't even trip on the stairs."

"Mmm...you are delicious." Strait's cock was out, and he was stroking it with slow, sure motions. "And all mine."

His mouth went dry, and it took him a second to speak. "All yours." He went right to Strait, dropped the lube and condoms on the couch and reached for that gorgeous cock. "Is this for me?"

"Every inch of it." Strait reached out, petting his tingling ass.

The touch made him stumble a little and tip over into Strait. "Oh, that's...thank you, Sir." He shifted, snatched the lube up off the couch and straddled his lover's thighs. That alone stretched him pretty wide, and he hummed happily as he circled his thumb over the thick cock Strait was still stroking slowly.

"Mmm...look at you." Strait's gaze was like a touch. "All hard and wanting for me. Get yourself slick, baby. I want to make you come on my cock."

His cowboy was surrounded by the lovely haze of his need-blurred vision, and he nodded. Anything Strait wanted. Anything.

He got his fingers all slippery and pushed up on his knees so he could reach better, groaning shamelessly and arching as he pushed two fingers inside. "Want you, Sir. So bad."

"Mmm... You'll have me." Strait put the condom on, that heavy cock hard as diamonds.

"Now?" He walked his knees in close and reached behind him again to get hold of Strait and guide him inside. He was so ready. He didn't want to wait another second.

"Now." Strait balanced him, holding his hips. He could feel the heat of the heavy prick as it pushed against his hole, Strait encouraging him down.

The stretch was delicious. He didn't intend to tease, but he savored that moment before the thick head slipped past his hole because it felt so good, working it just to the edge before pulling up again.

Strait seemed willing to let him enjoy, the expression on the beloved face fond. The hands still led him though, tight.

"You just feel so good, Sir." He lowered his hips, taking Strait in this time, not afraid to let his lover hear him gasp and moan as Strait filled him.

"Uhn." That soft, strangled sound was, without a doubt, an agreement. "More."

"Mmm. Yeah?" He loved that Strait was impatient, enough that he took his time, determined to drive his lover mad. He was on top right now, wasn't he? He could be just a little naughty.

Blunt nails dragged over his tenderized ass. "Yes, baby."

He hissed, reminded that naughty had its price. But he'd pay it willingly for the look in Strait's eyes. "Sir." He took the hungry cock in deep, until his warmed ass sat flat against Strait's thighs. He paused there a second. "Better?"

"You feel like heaven, baby. I can feel you, rippling all around my prick."

He nodded, taking a breath before he started to move again. "I want you to feel good." Assuming he could keep it together that long.

"Uh-huh." Strait added his strength to Tad's, dragging him up and down on his cock.

"Oh, fuck." Right. On top didn't mean in charge. He picked up Strait's pace, groaning with the burn and reaching for his own neglected prick.

"You don't come until I give you leave. I want this to last." Strait was beginning to flush, to punch in every time he dropped down.

Shit. Part of him wanted to cheer about the way Strait slid into this role so well, so naturally. Part of him wanted to scream. He pulled his hand away. "Yes, Sir."

He was mostly cheering.

He didn't have to twiddle his thumbs while he waited though. The next time he slid down and took Strait in deep, he clenched before he pulled back up. It made his eyes cross, and he moaned with the effort. Strait felt enormous inside him.

"Yeah... Fuck, baby. Do that again." That was a growl— nothing more than a deep, rough rumble.

He did what Strait asked but this time his lover hit just the right spot inside and he grunted, clenching even harder and breathing in deep. He couldn't come yet. Not yet. "Fuck…"

"Mmm…right there. I'm on it." Strait hit that spot unerringly.

"No, no. I mean, yes, but wait! That's good but I…oh fuck. Please." He didn't know what he was saying, he was babbling, and he had no control over what Sir wanted to do. He was aching, burning, he *needed*. Tad focused hard on keeping control, which took all his energy. "Please, please."

"Yes, baby. Come for me. Come on my cock." Those nails dragged over his ass again.

He gasped, fingers digging into Sir's shoulders as he shot almost instantly. It rocked him hard, and he knew he was shaking as he tried to give his Sir everything he had.

Strait rolled him to the sofa, slamming into him, driving him into the cushions, face drawn tight with his need. Those dark eyes burned down at him, watching him as Strait came.

That was something no one would ever see again but him. Because Strait was his now, forever. He caught his lover around the hips with his knees and held him and drew fingers over Strait's damp forehead. "Fuck. So good. You're so beautiful, Sir. Love you so much."

"Love. Love you, baby. Forever." The kiss he got was sloppy and rough.

"Forever." He returned the kiss, every breathless, sloppy, exhausted bit of it. It was perfect.

14

The island was beautiful, it really was the most amazing place Tad had ever been. He understood why Strait loved it so much—Strait was at his most creative, he was most relaxed, he even slept better there. And a couple of weeks in that creative space had allowed them to work on their relationship too, who they were together. He hadn't expected it to be so...amazing. Tad liked the island for that.

He knew he was going to have to figure things out. They were going home for now, but they'd be back, and Strait deserved to enjoy his sanctuary, and to work when he was inspired, without worrying that Tad was unhappy.

He figured this was the hard part of the whole committed relationship thing, and he was very willing but had no idea how to compromise. And really, Strait was everything to him. Maybe his lover shouldn't have to.

Maybe he was being selfish.

Still, he'd been lonely and unsure, and he'd wanted Strait to...to notice.

He moved a little closer as they waited for their bags and

let his fingers brush against his lover's. He knew he wasn't the only one thinking. It had been a quiet flight.

"You happy to be home, baby?" Strait rolled his shoulders, his back creaking.

Was the truth a bad thing? "Yes. I miss the dogs, and Mitch and Andy. Is that weird?" He missed Cooper too, but it wasn't like he saw Cooper as much living out where he did now.

"Those puppies are going to be big as houses. And why would enjoying coming home be weird. That's—well, that's why it's home."

"It is home, you know. It feels like home. I miss it like it's home. I guess that's what I meant by weird. I better see about getting out of my lease, huh? I won't be needing my apartment anymore." He smiled. It was nice to have a home with Strait.

"We ought to, yeah. And we'll hire someone to move you, if you want." Strait gave him a wicked grin. "I got a car to drive us home. You want to stop for some food?"

He grinned right back. "Something totally not tropical?"

"Fuck yes. Tacos or greasy burgers?" Strait winked at him, goosing him not-exactly gently.

He managed to contain his yelp to a shocked squeak and nodded. "Yes. Any of those things. All of them." The island was great, and they ate well. Really well. But literally everything was good for them. From the fresh pineapple to the fresh fish...he was craving junk food.

"Whataburger then. I'm dying for a patty melt, fries, and a strawberry shake."

He nodded, mouth watering. "Green chile double, fries, and a chocolate malt." He laughed, loving how they were so on the same page. "Oh. My bag."

"I'll grab it." Strait hauled the bag over, then grabbed his own bag. "The driver should be here by now."

Strait tickled the shit out of him. He had a private jet, but he didn't mind flying. He had a driver, but he could get his own bags, thank you. He had a security team that followed him everywhere, and Tad never saw them.

He followed Strait, dragging his suitcase along and smiling like he had any right to be this stupid happy. It was nice to know whatever they were each working out in their heads was easily tabled in favor of food and the promise of a snuggle in the car.

"Hey, Mr. Bill!" Strait chuckled and hugged the older gentleman in his redneck tuxedo. "How goes it?"

"Good. We've missed you. Delilah made you some pralines."

"Oh, y'all spoil me. This is my man, Tad. Tad, this is the husband of the prettiest woman in Houston, I swear to God."

My man. Best introduction ever. "Sounds like you're almost as lucky as I am, Mr. Bill." Tad shook the man's hand. "Good to meet you."

"Pleasure. Are you ready to hit the road? I brought the Hummer."

"We need Whataburger on the way out of town, yeah?"

Bill nodded, touched his ear and frowned. "Time to get you moving, Mr. Strait. Mr. Tad."

Suddenly they were almost running, heading out for a black Humvee, and he was breathless when the heavy door shut behind them.

He took a second to let the dust settle and then looked at Strait, brow furrowed. "Okay. I'll bite. What was that about?"

Strait blinked up. "Who knows? Some sort of threat that

made the team uncomfortable. I trust them to deal with that sort of thing."

"The team." Good fucking god. Every time he turned around Strait had more...people. He didn't actually care himself—Strait could be broke as long as he got to climb into those arms every night. The rest was fun, and he sure wasn't complaining but...wow. "So, I really don't have a full appreciation of exactly how big a celebrity you are, do I?"

"Not famous, just wealthy. Fame sounds like a pain in the ass. Money comes with its own shit—kidnapping threats are a thing."

"Well, shit, Strait. I'm never letting go of your hand again. Ever." He laughed. He kind of felt sorry for anyone that would try to kidnap his cowboy. He didn't think he'd want to tangle with Strait that way.

"Mmm...promise?" Strait pulled him close, nibbling below his ear.

Oh, that tickled. "Yes," he said through a soft giggle. "I promise. Never, ever."

"Good boy." Strait stroked his thigh. "So, did you like the island? I spend a few months a year there, so..."

"So...we're probably going back?" He grinned at Strait. "It is breathtaking. Beautiful. The clear water, the blue sky, the nearly empty beach, your amazing house..." The yacht and that pool and all the food. "The *sun*. Wow."

"I know you felt isolated, though. I don't want you miserable there."

"I know, Sir. And I don't want you to be worrying about me there either. You have to be able to do your thing and not be distracted by me whining about feeling lonely in such an amazing place." It did seem pretty ungrateful when he put it that way, honestly. "So, I'm thinking about next time. I want to be...prepared."

"That sounds fair. What does that mean, practically?" Strait listened to him like he was truly interested, like Tad mattered more than anything.

"I don't know yet. I guess I need a hobby. Or maybe... maybe Cooper could come for a few days? I don't know. I have to think." Cooper would shit little pink Twinkies all over the pristine sand.

"That would be fine with me. You're welcome to invite people. I would ask that you keep them out of my office space. You're welcome there, but no one else is."

"Of course. They're not going anywhere near our bedroom either." He glanced up at Strait. "Really, Sir? A visit would be okay? You're sure?" A few days tops. He wouldn't let anybody overstay their welcome. "Maybe we should have a couple of my friends out to the ranch first. Make sure you're okay with them? The island probably isn't the best place for a dry run." His friends were crazy, but they were respectful. Still, Strait should maybe talk to them before they showed up on...in that space. There was something really personal about that island for Strait that he hadn't understood at all until he'd been there and seen it for himself.

"Of course. It's your home too. We should have a cook-out, invite them out. If they're not nice, we'll let the dogs eat them."

He laughed, stretching up to kiss Strait's chin. "That works. Or, if they're not nice you can threaten them with your team. Do they have dark glasses too? Cooper has a thing for guys in sunglasses."

"We have a security manager, and he deals with the guys. I just go when they say I need to. I grew up with security, you know? Even at football games."

"That's wild. I like the idea of a barbecue. That would be fun." His buddies, the pool, the sun, some beer...oh yeah. That would be a good time.

"Good deal. The guys would be happy to bartend for us. I want to introduce you to my people too. They're gonna need to meet you before the wedding, I think. Maybe Sunday we can go for supper."

He nodded. "That's terrifying, but I can't wait." He knew they were good people, and the way Strait talked about them, it was obvious he was fond of them, but meeting parents was still a big deal. "I'm ready."

"Excellent." Strait watched him like a hawk. "So, to-do list—Whataburger, party for friends, supper with Granny and them, wild monkey sex, get your apartment packed, love on puppies."

"Hm. There's not enough sex on that list. And you forgot a good spanking and some super-toppy growling. I'm sure I'll deserve it at some point." For being bad, or for being good. Either way worked for him.

"A good spanking, hmm? I seem to remember you reacted to those well." Strait's voice went low, a little husky, making him shiver.

"Really? You'll have to remind me, Sir." Anytime. All the time. Right now. He was easy.

Strait chuckled softly, the sound surprisingly wicked. "I have plans for you, baby. Don't you worry."

What? Plans? His eyes popped open wide at the shiver that went up his spine and the ache in his balls. "You do? I mean—yes, Sir. That sounds good to me."

"I do. I have a box waiting for me at home. I'll introduce it to you. Later."

A box. Later. This was more exciting than Christmas. He

almost suggested they skip Whataburger, but they needed to eat, and he was excited about junk food too.

Strait winked at him. "We're going to have so much fun, you and me and my 3D printer."

EPILOGUE

Underneath his cutoffs, Tad was wearing his diving suit. He intended to swim later, after the party died down a little and some of the company had gone home. Right now, though, he was carrying four bottles of beer and headed right past the pool toward his friends who were all craning their necks and looking around like they were at Disney World instead of in his backyard.

"Beer!" Cooper took two and handed one to Rory, and Tad handed one to Juanito.

He couldn't help smiling, he loved having his friends here. "Everyone settled in?"

"There have to be two hundred people here, man. And —Is that Austin Majors?" Cooper's eyes were huge.

He glanced over, nodded. The movie star was actually a gentle, sweet man who had been madly in love with the man Strait had buried the day they met. "He's a good guy."

There were easily two hundred people. And if Strait hadn't put his foot down—gently and respectfully—with his mother there might have been four hundred.

"Who are those folks over there?" Rory pointed with his chin.

Tad followed Rory's gaze to the "Well, I don't know them really but the gentleman with the beard is Strait's father."

"Damn, Tad. He's handsome."

"Right?" He thought Strait looked more like his mother though.

"So you're really going on a month-long honeymoon? Like a whole month?" Cooper looked utterly stunned. "And he told you anywhere you wanted?"

"He promised me a month and the northern lights." He didn't think they'd be in the frozen north for a month, though, and he had no idea where Strait planned to take him after that. "The rest is up to him."

"Spoiled." Rory, every toppy inch of him, scanned the party like he was looking for an easy mark.

"I am. No question."

"Tad!" He turned to look for the voice and saw Strait standing with his mom and waving him over.

"Uh-oh, you're being summoned by Himself," Cooper teased.

"Shut up. You guys should check out the grills, everything looks amazing. I'll be back."

Cooper goosed him as he walked away, and he held in a yelp. He was still a little sore from last night's paddling.

Strait hadn't lied a bit about that 3D printer. It was obscene what his Dom could create with that thing. Tad was a lucky, lucky man.

"Hello, my dear." Olivia smiled at him, kissed his cheek. She had accepted him, folded her in without question. Strait's dad? That had taken a little longer. "I'm sorry to interrupt, but Granny is not going to want to stay too much longer, and you know how she adores you."

He gave her a great big smile because she deserved it, and because it had taken him no time at all to love her. "Hi, Momma. You look so pretty! I definitely don't want to disappoint Granny. I'll head right over." Granny was the oldest woman on the planet, and the smartest. Strait's dad was a little intimidating, but he sure wouldn't mess with Granny.

"Hey, you! It's getting loud for me, and I'm going to take my old bones home. Are you having a nice party? I want to give you my engagement present." She pressed an envelope into his hand. "This is yours. Not my grandson's. Do you understand me?"

He took the envelope and looked at it, then back at her. "You're too good to me, Granny. You don't have to give me a gift."

"I know. That's why I gave it to you." She patted his cheek. "You're coming to supper tomorrow night? Evelyn is making fried chicken."

"You know it. I'm looking forward to our card game." He'd lose, again. She was a shark.

"That's my boy. Go enjoy your party. Kiss that grandboy for me. Love you, honey."

"I will. I'm going to kiss you first though, so don't let anybody see you blush." He kissed her on the cheek and gave her a smile. "Love you. Thank you for this. See you tomorrow." He waved and wandered off, feeling ridiculously loved even if his own parents declined his invitation.

He managed to find a spot to sit by the pool and opened his envelope. He'd expected a little money, that seemed like a reasonable gift from a grandparent, but he didn't pull out a check.

It took him a minute to figure out what it was, but he

finally saw the legend. It was a deed for land in Jackson Hole, and a picture of a sweet little cabin.

What? A cabin? He looked over his shoulder to where he'd left Granny, but she was gone. He looked back at the deed, turning it over in his fingers like it couldn't be real.

Strait came over to him, always so attuned to him. "You okay, baby boy?"

He looked up at Strait and reached for his hand. "Granny gave me an engagement present."

Strait looked over the paper, then smiled. "You'll have to take me up there, show me around."

He laughed. "Are you kidding me? Granny gave me a cabin! We're spending part of our honeymoon there. We have to. I want to bring back pictures, tell her how amazing it is." He stood and slipped an arm around Strait's waist. "Did you know?"

"I knew she wanted you to have something that was only yours, something of value. I didn't know more than that." Strait bent to kiss him. "You ought to go put that away, baby, then come out and party."

"Yes, Sir. I promised myself I'd talk to your dad. And then I want some of Mitch's barbecue."

"Good deal." Strait winked at him, gave him that grin. "Save me a dance, baby. I love you."

"You get all my dances, love." His handsome cowboy, lover, Dom. Everything.

No more wondering who he was spending the night with. His cowboy had laid his claim, and Tad was taken, balls to bones.

Sin Deep
By Jodi Payne and BA Tortuga

Winter Love knows how to give. He gave himself his own name after all, and he's given love to many young men who later moved on with someone they wanted more. Too many. So he's stopped putting himself out there to be hurt by the young little birds he prefers, though he does still enjoy going to the gentlemen's club where he has a membership. He's older, old-fashioned, eccentric, and content to be more about people watching these days.

Harley McBride is new to New York City, having left his home in Texas for a more welcoming town. He's hard-working, friendly, and has a curious nature, which means he's having a great time meeting people. When his roommate takes him to an interesting new club, he decides to introduce himself to a man who is fascinating to him, even from across the room.

Caught off-guard, Winter takes a chance in return, and asks Harley to let him make up Harley's dark eyes. Things begin to heat up, and the two of them connect in ways that neither of them could have anticipated. But Winter knows he needs to tread carefully, and Harley is used to being independent and handling things on his own. Will they be able to find a path that suits them both, or will their relationship stay simply sin deep?

Buy it now or read in KU!

Interested in learning more about BA's cowboys and Jodi's gentlemen? Want free fiction and news? Join our newsletters!

What's Up with Jodi
http://bit.ly/whatsupjodi

Spurs and Shifters
https://lp.constantcontact.com/su/A9CRUzp/baandjulia

Howdy, Y'all!

We want to thank you for giving Temptation Ranch a try. We hope you enjoyed the story.

If you can spare a few minutes to post a review at the retail website where you made your purchase, we'd very much appreciate it!

Don't forget to "like" our Facebook pages and groups to keep up with all the news--new releases, sales announcements, giveaways, sneak peeks-- and of course the rodeo pictures, coffee memes and just general fun. We'd love to have all y'all!

Yeehaw and thanks for reading!

BA & Jodi

ABOUT JODI

JODI takes herself way too seriously and has been known to randomly break out in song. Her men are imperfect but genuine, stubborn but likable, often kinky, and frequently their own worst enemies. They are characters you can't help but fall in love with while they stumble along the path to their happily ever after. For those looking to get on her good side, Jodi's addictions include nonfat lattes, Malbec and tequila any way you pour it.

Website: jodipayne.net
Newsletter: https://readerlinks.com/l/2317334
All Jodi's Social Links: linktr.ee/jodipayne

ABOUT BA

Western to the bone and an unrepentant Daddy's Girl, BA Tortuga spends her days with her hounds and her beloved wife, having mother-daughter dates, and eating Mexican food. When she's not doing that, she's writing. She spends her days off watching rodeo, knitting, and surfing Pinterest in the name of research. Following their own personal joys, BA and Julia heard the call of the high desert and they now live in the New Mexico mountains. BA's personal saviors include her wife, her best friends, and coffee. Lots of coffee. Really good coffee.

Having written everything from fist-fighting cowboys to rural single dads to werewolves, BA does her damnedest to tell the stories of her heart, which is committed to giving everyone their happily ever after. With books ranging from heart-warming stories of found families, to rodeo cowboys that are fighting to make a mark, to fiery passionate love affairs, BA refuses to be pigeon-holed by anyone but the voices in her head.

BA loves to talk to her readers and can be found at http://batortuga.com/ and her newsletter signup link is http://bit.ly/BAJulianews

AVAILABLE FROM JODI & BA

The Cowboy and the Dom Trilogy

First Rodeo, Book One

Razor's Edge, Book Two

No Ghosts, Book Three

The Soldier and the Angel, a Cowboy and Dom Novel

Sin Deep, a Cowboy and Dom Novel

East Meets Westerns

(single titles)

Wrecked

Flying Blind

Special Delivery, A Wrecked Holiday Novel

Temptation Ranch

The Merry Everything Series

Window Dressing

Cowboy Protection

The Higher Elevation Series

Heart of a Cowboy

Land of Enchantment

Keeping Promises

Bigger Than Us

Home Free

The Triskelion Series

Breaking the Rules

Making a Mark

Making the Rules

Les's Bar Series

Just Dex

Hide Bound

Wholly Trinity

The Lone Star Series

Tending Tyler

Roped In

The Collaborations Series

Refraction

Syncopation

Puzzles Series

Cryptic

www.ingramcontent.com/pod-product-compliance
Lightning Source LLC
Chambersburg PA
CBHW032011240626
47153CB00003B/1202